"I wondered if I might be able to hire you."

Ivey felt her cheeks flush. Why had that sounded flirtatious? She added in a hurry, "To help me with some work around here. I need someone with some muscle to drag out mattresses and beat the dust out of them."

The words came out sounding almost intimate. What had gotten into her?

Cully's lazy smile stayed in place.

"So, anyway," she said, "I'm sure you're busy, but do you think you could spare a day? I'll pay whatever you want…."

"Around here we don't have to be paid to help out a neighbor."

"Still, I'd feel better if I could compensate you," she said.

His smile broadened and turned a touch mischievous. "Did you have somethin' besides money in mind?"

She wanted to crawl into a hole. *I've gone crazy,* she thought. *Completely out of my mind….*

Dear Reader,

Those long days of summer sunshine are just around the corner—and Special Edition has six fabulous new books to start off the season right!

This month's THAT'S MY BABY! title is brought to you by the wonderful Janis Reams Hudson. *His Daughter's Laughter* tells the poignant tale of a widowed dad, his fragile little girl and the hope they rediscover when one extraordinary woman touches their lives.

June is the month of wedding bells—or in some cases, wedding blues. Be sure to check out the plight of a runaway bride who leaves one groom behind, only to discover another when she least expects it in *Cowboy's Lady*—the next installment in Victoria Pade's ongoing A RANCHING FAMILY miniseries. And there's more romance on the way with award-winning author Ruth Wind's *Marriage Material*—book one in THE LAST ROUNDUP, a new cross-line series with Intimate Moments about three brothers who travel the rocky road to love in a small Colorado town.

And speaking of turbulent journeys, in *Remember Me?* Jennifer Mikels tells a passionate love story about an amnesiac woman who falls for the handsome hero who rescues her from a raging rainstorm. Also in June, Shirley Larson presents *That Wild Stallion*—an emotional Western that's sure to tug your heartstrings.

Finally, *New York Times* bestselling author Ellen Tanner Marsh lives up to her reputation with *A Doctor in the House,* her second Silhouette title. It's all work and no play for this business executive until he meets his match in the form of one feisty Southern beauty in the Florida Keys!

I hope you enjoy all our summer stories this month!

Sincerely,

Tara Gavin
Senior Editor

Please address questions and book requests to:
Silhouette Reader Service
U.S.: 3010 Walden Ave., P.O. Box 1325, Buffalo, NY 14269
Canadian: P.O. Box 609, Fort Erie, Ont. L2A 5X3

VICTORIA PADE

COWBOY'S LADY

Silhouette®

SPECIAL EDITION®

Published by Silhouette Books

America's Publisher of Contemporary Romance

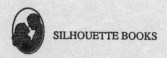 SILHOUETTE BOOKS

ISBN 0-373-24106-2

COWBOY'S LADY

Books by Victoria Pade

Silhouette Special Edition

Breaking Every Rule #402
Divine Decadence #473
Shades and Shadows #502
Shelter from the Storm #527
Twice Shy #558
Something Special #600
Out on a Limb #629
The Right Time #689
Over Easy #710
Amazing Gracie #752
Hello Again #778
Unmarried with Children #852
*Cowboy's Kin #923
*Baby My Baby #946
*Cowboy's Kiss #970
Mom for Hire #1057
*Cowboy's Lady #1106

*A Ranching Family

VICTORIA PADE

is a bestselling author of both historical and contemporary romance fiction, and mother of two energetic daughters, Cori and Erin. Although she enjoys her chosen career as a novelist, she occasionally laments that she has never traveled farther from her Colorado home than Disneyland, instead spending all her spare time plugging away at her computer. She takes breaks from writing by indulging in her favorite hobby—eating chocolate.

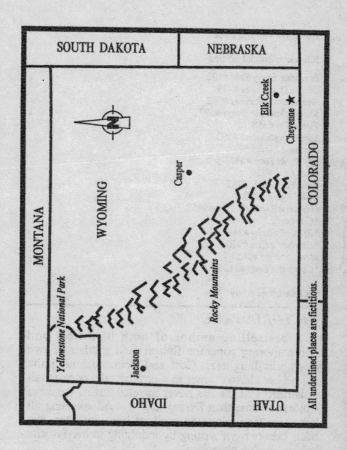

All underlined places are fictitious.

Prologue

Ivey Heller's wedding dress was an elaborate array of antique lace and hand-sewn pearls over cream-colored satin, with an ankle-length veil and a yard-long train. The high collar wrapped her neck, the bodice molded her breasts and shaped a waist narrow enough to make any Southern belle jealous. It was the image of what she'd always dreamed of wearing.

A last glance in the church's dressing room mirror told her she looked exactly the way she wanted to look, exactly the way a bride should look.

The natural curls of her strawberry blond hair had sprung to life all around her face and down to just past her shoulders. Her violet eyes didn't give away the fact that she'd spent nearly every night for the last week without much sleep. And with the help of the makeup artist her fiancé had hired, she had on just enough eye shadow, liner, mascara, blush and lipstick to enhance and highlight the assets of her features and draw attention away from what she considered her flaws—a few freckles across the bridge of a too perky nose and lips that were on the pale side.

Now if only she could get rid of that scared-doe look that reflected back at her from the mirror.

Two knocks on the door just then were her signal that it was time to get this show on the road.

A chill ran up her spine and made her shiver all over.

But she ignored it, told herself to cut it out, and went from the dressing room into the church's lobby.

She stepped to within a scant few feet of the entrance to the nave—off to the side so she couldn't be seen from the interior—and took a good look at what awaited her.

The church was decorated beautifully in tiny white baby's breath flowers and yellow rosebuds that sent their sweet smell all the way out to her. Guests filled every pew, dressed in their best. A string quartet played Vivaldi's "Spring" from *The Four Seasons*—not too loud, not too soft, every note just right. Just the way she'd always dreamed it would be.

Even the weather outside on that early Friday evening was balmy—seventy degrees, with a bare hint of autumn in the October air. She couldn't have asked for better.

Not far away, her sister, Savannah, fussed over the flower girl and the ring bearer, and Ivey and Savannah's cousins—Linc and Jackson Heller—waited to walk Ivey down the aisle, both of them decked out in tuxedos.

If they had any qualms about giving her away to Arlen Earl Brunswell, it didn't show.

But then, why would anyone have any qualms about

her marrying Arlen Earl Brunswell? After all, he was the youngest-ever president of one of Cheyenne's biggest banks. A man from a wealthy family of long standing in Wyoming's social and political circles. A man whom a local magazine had named first choice for most attractive, most eligible bachelor. The catch of the decade.

And the wedding that was about to begin had been touted as the social event of the season. Why, even the mayor and the governor were guests.

So Ivey should have been the happiest woman in the world and she reminded herself of that fact as she watched from the distance and saw Arlen step to his place just in front of the chancel rail, his best man at one elbow, the minister at his other.

The magazine had been right, he was an attractive man. Refined features, impeccably cut brown hair, five feet ten inches and not an ounce of fat on him. He stood straight, proud, confident.

So why didn't she hear bells and whistles at that initial sight of him? The bells and whistles she'd always thought she would hear when she set eyes on the man she loved enough to marry.

But the truth was, she didn't hear them. She hadn't heard them the whole time they'd been together....

She saw Arlen glance at his wristwatch as if she were late for an appointment with him and suddenly in her mind it was something else she heard.

What was it he'd called her most of the evening before at the rehearsal dinner?

My little ball-and-chain-to-be, that was it.

Ha, ha, ha...

Fast on that came more memories of things Arlen

had said during the last few months of wedding preparations.

*Don't worry, for a wedding gift I'm giving you some
class....*

*She only teaches kindergarten because she's not
smart enough to teach first grade....*

*We're quite a couple—the bank president and his
little country hick....*

All fluff, no brains...

Ha, ha, ha...

Arlen thought he was a pretty funny guy. And it
seemed as if every day the wedding had drawn closer,
every day that he'd become more secure in the knowledge that she was his, the more funny he'd felt free to
be.

The only problem was that Ivey didn't find his comments quite as riotous as he did. They erupted all sorts
of old, unpleasant emotions in her. They made her feel
like dirt.

And she'd told him so. Asked him to be more con-
siderate of her feelings, more sensitive. More respectful.

*Crybaby. Can't take a few jokes. Maybe we can buy
you a sense of humor when we shop for new clothes
to replace all that bad taste you're wearing now....*

Ha, ha, ha...

Not that Arlen wasn't a decent enough man. Hardworking. Smart. Successful. Well thought of. He sent
cards and flowers on birthdays, on Valentine's Day. He
remembered the anniversaries of the day they'd met,
the day they'd gotten engaged. He had flawless manners and he could be fun to be with when he wasn't
making her the butt of his humor.

But where were those bells and whistles? And why

didn't they go off even when he held her in his arms? Even when he kissed her? Even when he did more than kiss her?

She'd been listening for them. Wishing for them. Trying hard to conjure them up.

But not once, not a single time, had anything about Arlen Earl Brunswell caused her to hear them. Or to feel more than a pleasant contentment at his touch, his kiss, his company.

Maybe if she could just get him to stop making those jokes...

Or maybe that bells and whistles thing was just some romantic fantasy. Not something that really happened. Not something to base her future on. Not something to throw away a man like Arlen Earl Brunswell for because she didn't hear them.

She'd have a good life with him. Everybody said so. A nice house. Kids. Travel. A husband with a sense of humor...

Till death do we part...

Till death do we part...

Why did that phrase echo in her mind all of a sudden? Goad her, even?

And why was her heart beating so hard and fast she could hear it, drowning out the music coming from inside the church? Why was her stomach in such a tight knot it ached? And why couldn't she draw a decent breath? Why was she suddenly pulling in short gasps that made her head spin and spots of light appear before her eyes?

"You all right, darlin'?" her cousin Linc asked as he and Jackson stepped to either side of her, closing a big hand around her arm to steady her.

"She's hyperventilating," she heard Jackson answer

his brother when she couldn't do any more than wheeze short hiccups of air.

It drew quite a commotion that she couldn't seem to avoid, even though she tried to wave everyone away. Linc and Jackson, Savannah, the ushers, the dressmaker who'd been fiddling with her train, the flower arranger standing nearby to hand her her bouquet, all gathered around her.

"Make her breathe into a paper bag," somebody said.

"Who has a paper bag?" someone else asked.

"I'll find one," yet another promised.

I'm going to die, Ivey thought. *Right here, in the church, in my wedding gown, on my wedding day. Feeling like an idiot. Like the stupid, weak, wimpy, silly, foolish female my father...and Arlen...said I was...*

But still she couldn't catch her breath and her head was getting lighter. Spinning uncontrollably. Her knees were weak. Her body was as heavy as lead. Her eyes were open, only now she couldn't see anything but the spots of light and she really did think she might be dying.

She didn't want to die....

On the other hand, she thought as her knees buckled and she felt herself falling to the floor, at least if she did, she wouldn't have to be anybody's ball and chain....

Chapter One

It had been a long time since Ivey had been in Elk Creek—the small Wyoming town in which she'd grown up. A long time since she'd been at her uncle's ranch just outside of town.

But her uncle's guest room—actually, it was her cousin Jackson's guest room now—was where she woke up before dawn the next morning. Alone. Unmarried. An escapee from the social event of the season.

With a heavy weight on her conscience.

She didn't regret not going through with the wedding. But she wasn't proud of slipping out the back door of the church, letting Savannah, Linc and Jackson deal with Arlen and the guests. Even if it had been their idea because Savannah was afraid of the kind of uproar Arlen might make if Ivey herself announced that she wasn't going through with marrying him. Softening the blow was what her sister had had in mind.

But still Ivey had felt like a thief in the night, slinking out to avoid the repercussions of her actions.

Her father—if he were still alive—would have called her the worst kind of coward. Among other things. And that was exactly how Ivey thought of herself as she lay awake in the dark room feeling guilty and confused. Very, very confused.

She could hardly believe that she—a quiet, conservative, by-the-books kindergarten teacher—had left Arlen Earl Brunswell waiting at the altar. How could she have done such a thing?

Embarrassing them both in front of everyone they knew. Squandering all the money they'd spent on the wedding. Hurting Arlen...

Had she hurt Arlen?

Surely she must have. And yet it was difficult for her to imagine that she had the power to strike any kind of real emotional blow.

Oh, he'd be hopping mad. Furious for being humiliated with all those people there to see it. Enraged at the unbelievable audacity of *her* dumping *him*.

But would he feel anything remotely like pain or sadness?

She just couldn't picture it. Because, she realized with a sadness of her own, she'd never had the sense that she was that important to him. That she'd been anything more than an ornament he'd decided to decorate himself with because he'd reached a stage in his life when it seemed to be the time for marrying, starting a family.

But had he cared about her as a person? As the woman she was inside?

She wished she could believe that he did. But she couldn't. He didn't even know her as a person or as the woman she was inside.

He didn't listen to her when she talked; he actually told her she was better seen and not heard even when they were alone. He didn't ask anything about her beyond a perfunctory *How was your day?* and he never heard what she said about it when she answered. He'd talked about himself almost constantly and then he'd gone on to something else—to sleep, to watch television, to read a book, to do work he'd brought with him, never to hear her out.

So how had she thought she could spend the rest of her life like that? As a part of the woodwork?

It amazed her now to think she had.

The rest of her life...

Till death do we part...

That had been the trigger that had sent her into such a tailspin and ultimately led her to running out on the wedding. And it brought her up short on finding fault with Arlen.

He might not have made a good husband. He might not have been a very sensitive person. But she couldn't deny her own part in yesterday's fiasco.

Could she be commitment-shy? she wondered now.

She had to admit to the possibility. After all, here she was, thirty-three years old, and Arlen had been the first long-term relationship she'd ever had, the first man she'd actually let get close. And hadn't it been that eternity thing that had freaked her out? What was that if not a fear of making a lifelong commitment?

Great, she thought, *so what do we have here? I'm commitment-phobic with lousy judgment in men.*

What a mess. What a great big mess. And she'd

thought she was so levelheaded, so together, so sure-footed.

Instead maybe she was just the good-for-nothing, waste of space and air that her father...and Arlen, in his own way...had said she was.

Ivey groaned and pulled the covers over her face.

Maybe it wasn't a good idea to have come back to Elk Creek, she thought suddenly, as if just being in the vicinity of her childhood was enough to make her feel as down on herself as she had as a kid, as her father had made her feel.

Not that Elk Creek wasn't a nice little town itself. It was. But it hadn't been the site of a happy time for her or for Savannah, and leaving it had seemed like a way to shed the effects of being raised by the irascible, hard-as-nails Silas Heller.

And here she was back again, feeling more rotten and worthless than she had since she'd left.

Well, she wasn't going to let it get the better of her, she decided, flinging the covers down again.

She'd made a bad choice in Arlen Earl Brunswell, and she shouldn't have let things get all the way to the wedding ceremony before she called it quits—she'd take responsibility for all of that. But she wasn't going to let those mistakes throw her back fifteen years whether she was in Elk Creek or not.

Silas wasn't around anymore to build her every fault out of proportion and she wasn't going to do it to her-self, that was for sure.

Hints of sunshine were nudging their way around the edges of the drapes, and although Ivey couldn't explain it to save her life, she felt drawn to that old house across the road, to seeing it again, maybe to testing her own ability to face the memories it held, to stand up to them. Since it wasn't likely that she was going to be able to sleep anymore, she got out of bed, thinking that she might as well do it all now as later.

She took a plain T-shirt and a pair of jeans from the suitcase she'd had packed for her honeymoon and went into the bathroom connected to her room for a quick shower.

Fifteen years, she thought as she did.

That was how long it had been since she'd stepped foot in the house in which she and Savannah had grown up.

And now that that was where she was headed, she wondered how it would make her feel...

It was a long walk from the H-shaped, two-story house that Shag Heller had built, down the drive that led to it, across the road to the property Ivey and her sister had owned since their father's death.

For a moment she stood staring at the twenty-foot-tall wooden arch that proclaimed it the Double H Ranch as if it were the first time she'd seen it. The *U* in Double was missing, so now it was the Do ble H Ranch.

What exactly was do-able? Ivey wondered as she passed under the sign.

The house was a full half mile from the road, at the end of an unpaved, rutted path, and she walked it in no hurry to reach her destination, entertaining no sense of nostalgia whatsoever.

It was a stroll she'd taken many times as a child, coming home from visits to her cousins, and later from being with her friends. Friends who had always dropped her off at the road rather than venture all the

way up to the house and risk encountering her father.
It was a reluctance she'd shared.

The house came into view at a quarter of a mile and
it struck her anew how much smaller it was than
Shag's. But then, of the two brothers, Shag had been
the more successful, especially in his purchases of
property in town and his use of the land outside of it.

Ivey's father—Silas—had never expanded the original parcels he'd inherited from Ivey's grandfather, nor
added onto the house that had come with them—the
original home of Ivey's great-great-grandfather, one of
the earliest settlers of Elk Creek.

It was two-storied, too, but no match for the sprawling home of the other Hellers. No, the house Ivey had
grown up in looked like any ordinary farmhouse.

The lower level was clapboard—faded from its once
white color to a rusty ecru now, and fronted by a covered porch that stuck out like a pouter's lip.

The second story was really more like an attic space,
set the way it was completely in the shingled slope of
the roof, with dormer windows poking out of it, two
each on all four sides.

The place was not in good shape. Shutters hung
askew, their black paint peeling away to old gray wood.
The roof was bald in spots where shingles were missing. And the front screen door was hanging by a single
hinge as if the wind had caught it but it had hung on
for dear life.

None of the glass was broken out of the windows
but they were all clouded over with grime. And as she
drew closer she could see the dirt blown into small
dunes on the porch floor.

One of the wooden steps that rose up to that floor
was broken out, but that wasn't what kept Ivey from

climbing them when she got that far. It was thoughts of a childhood spent with a humorless man who hadn't been happy to have daughters rather than sons, who was left alone to raise them when his wife deserted them all.

But Ivey was determined not to let the place or the memories that went with it get the better of her this morning, so she forced herself to climb those stairs—skipping the broken one—and went up onto the porch.

The key was still in the mailbox and that made her smile. Fifteen years and no one had taken it, whether they'd used it or not. That wasn't something likely to happen in the city.

Ivey unlocked the heavy mahogany door with its oval glass in the upper half and stepped into the entryway. The soles of her loafers echoed hollowly on the hardwood floor as she went far enough in to close the door behind her. Then she leaned back against it to look around, to get her bearings, avoiding any thoughts of the part of her life she'd lived there.

To the left, riding the wall, was the staircase with its braided runner rising to the upper level. Straight ahead was a hall that stretched to the kitchen in the rear.

To her right was the living room and a glance in that direction told her that someone had used the house as a trysting site—respectfully, because nothing was damaged. But there was a blanket and some throw pillows set out before the fireplace, a few empty wine bottles lined up along the mantel, and burned candles here and there.

At least someone had made good use of the place, she thought.

Ivey pushed away from the door and turned into the living room, where the furniture was covered in sheets that had done their job collecting dust. From there she went across the similarly shrouded dining room and through the other entrance to the kitchen, all the while half expecting to encounter her father any minute even though she knew that wasn't possible.

Silas had been dead for all but two months of those fifteen years since Ivey and Savannah had left home, yet his presence in the house still seemed tangible. She even caught herself listening for sounds of him, the way she had as a kid, ready to alter her path to avoid him if she heard him coming.

But of course that didn't happen and by the time she made it to the kitchen she was feeling less tentative about being there.

Breathing the dust was getting to her, though, so she went out to the mudroom off the left side of the kitchen with its dated appliances and big, round, claw-footed table, and opened the door to let in some of the fresh morning air.

As she did she caught sight of someone going into the barn out back.

A man. A big man. And for a moment it flashed through her mind that it really was her father. But of course that couldn't be and, fast on the heels of that thought, came the realization that the man was probably one of the Culhane brothers.

The Culhane brothers owned the property next to hers, a much larger, working ranch. Through lawyers, she and Savannah rented them the barn and use of their land, too.

For the first time since Linc and Jackson had arrived in Cheyenne for the wedding, she remembered that Jackson had mentioned that the Culhanes wanted to buy Ivey and Savannah out. But in all the wedding commotion she and her sister hadn't even discussed it.

The man had left the barn's great door open so she could see him inside. Tall. Broad-shouldered. Long, slightly bowed legs.

He was dressed in the cowboy boots that were de rigueur in these parts, snug-fitting blue jeans, and a faded khaki-colored shirt. But she couldn't tell which of the three Culhanes he was.

The brothers had been rowdy, hell-raising heart-breakers. All of them good-looking, slightly older than she was, and uninterested in the mousy, tomboyish girl she'd been. As far as she could tell, none of them had even known she existed. Certainly to her knowledge they'd never given her the time of day.

But now a sense of courtesy urged her to go out and say hello.

Or maybe she was just looking for an excuse to get out of that dusty old house.

Either way, she opened the rickety screen door with its scant remnants of rusted screen hanging from the frame, stepped down the three naked stairs to the dry earth below and crossed the yard to the barn.

When she got there she stood in the span of the great door taking stock of the man. She still couldn't tell exactly which of the Culhane brothers he was. But that didn't surprise her. With the length of the barn still between them and fifteen years behind them, she didn't expect to know right off if he was Clint, Yance or Cully. Besides, there had always been a close resem-blance among the three and without having them all side by side she doubted she could even guess which this one was.

But whichever one he was, he'd ended up more than

six feet tall—probably a full three inches more. And big boned with one of those perfectly proportioned, boxy builds that looked so powerful and muscle-packed he seemed like a brick wall of a man.

He hadn't lost any of the good looks the Culhane brothers were notorious for, either, Ivey realized as she took a few steps into the barn. In fact, if anything, maturity had sharpened the planes and angles of his face and added to the appeal.

His hair was a shiny, sable brown that bordered on red in the highlights. He wore it close cut on the sides and back, the top slightly longer and combed carelessly away from his brow.

By halfway down the center aisle she could see his profile clearly. His features were starkly masculine. He had a high, square forehead and a nose that was a bit on the large side, although anything smaller wouldn't have fit his face. It was a no-nonsense nose, straight and just pointed enough at the end, with nostrils that angled upward.

His lips were full, but not so full as to be pouty, and there was a jut to his chiseled jawline and chin that somehow said they were strong enough to take a punch.

She couldn't for the life of her remember what color eyes the Culhane brothers all had. She could only recall that they had been the subject of swoons among those of her friends who were more mature and had fostered crushes on the brothers. Ivey hadn't been thinking about things like that then and so hadn't paid any attention.

But she wondered about it now. And the only way she was going to figure out which of the Culhanes he was or what color eyes they all had was to actually see his face. Since she was only two stalls away from him by then and he still hadn't heard her nearly soundless steps on the hard-packed dirt floor or seemed to even sense her presence, she said, "Good morning."

She hadn't meant to startle him but his head jolted up and he shouted, "What the hell?" in a deep, rich, angry voice.

"Whoops! I didn't mean to scare you."

"Then you shouldn't be sneakin' up on a man," he answered in no uncertain terms, reminding her of her father in that instant of gruffness.

Ivey closed the last few feet between them anyway. "I wasn't sneaking up on you. That's why I said good morning."

"Not until you were right on top of me."

An image of the two of them literally in that position popped into her mind and left her shocked at herself. Where had that come from? she wondered. But she only said, "You just must not have been expecting anyone."

"You got that right."

He gave her the once-over then and as he did she finally got a gander at his eyes. Glacial blue. Not the cornflower of her Heller cousins, but a blue so pale, so clear, they almost weren't any color at all. They looked like a cloudless winter sky reflected on ice.

Her friends had been right to swoon over them, she thought, amazed that even as a disinterested girl she had been able to ignore eyes that gorgeous.

"Who are you?" he demanded bluntly then.

"I didn't think you'd know me." They could have been bosom buddies fifteen years ago and he probably still wouldn't have recognized her. She'd changed that much. Purposely. "I'm Ivey Heller."

Thick eyebrows arched in surprise as he took a second look at her. A much closer, more appraising look that lingered here and there with what almost seemed to be a lazy appreciation.

Then, in his own good time, he settled those incredible eyes on her face once more and said more congenially, "What're you doin' here? I thought Linc and Jackson were goin' into Cheyenne to your wedding. Or couldn't you think of a better place than this for a honeymoon?"

His features had eased into a smooth, curious expression and he managed to put a titillating twist to the simple word *honeymoon.* And for some reason Ivey couldn't figure out, it made her feel flushed.

Maybe it was just embarrassment at even the mention of her aborted wedding.

"I didn't end up getting married," she informed him without going into any details and changed the subject back to what she was more interested in finding out. "And you still haven't returned the favor and told me which of the Culhane brothers you grew up to be."

"The same one I started out as." He touched a single, long, thick index finger to the brim of a hat that wasn't there and said, "Cully."

Ah, the youngest of the Culhane brothers, two years Ivey's senior.

"We sent word with Jackson about buying you folks out," he said then. "Is that why you're back? To make the deal?"

"No, it isn't. Savannah and I haven't had time to talk about that. And we'll need to."

"So you just came here instead of getting married? For no good reason? After—what's it been? Twelve, thirteen years?"

"Fifteen."

"Seems kind of strange," he said in a way that left an opening for her to explain.

But that was about the last thing she had any intention of doing. "Let's just say I was overdue for a visit," she said, not meaning it to come out so abrasively, but hearing the edge in her own voice that made her sound standoffish, crabby. So much for her sense of courtesy.

He frowned just barely in response, causing two vertical lines to form between his brows. But he didn't address her acid tongue. Instead he pointed his chin in the direction from which she'd come moments before, asking with a cooler tone to his own voice, "You staying in the house?"

Now there was a novel idea.

"I don't know," she said, surprised to find herself actually mulling it over suddenly. "Things are kind of up in the air with me right now. I'm not sure what I'm doing." Except that once more she sounded as if her back was up. What was wrong with her? Maybe her guilty conscience was making her defensive.

He nodded, keeping his ice blue eyes on her as if trying to read her.

It made her uncomfortable. Which spurred her to fill the silence by thinking out loud. "I suppose I could stay here a while. Sort through some things, get a handle on whether or not Savannah and I should hang on to the place or sell out..."

"Sounds like an idea," he said as if he couldn't care less one way or another what she did.

But then, why should he? And why should he put any more effort into making conversation with someone who kept intermittently biting his head off?

Trying to make some sort of amends, she opted for small talk. "Are you here every day?"

"Yep. Seeing to these animals."

"So I guess if I stick around we'll be running into each other."

"Guess we will be. Just holler out the next time so I have some warning." He turned his attention back to the mare he'd been grooming.

"Sure," she said, knowing she'd blown this as a friendly overture. She decided to cut her losses. "I'll just leave you to your work," she muttered to his broad back, unable to keep her eyes from riding along on the rise and fall of the taut muscles of his shoulders stretching the shirt he wore.

He didn't answer her so she just turned tail and headed out of the barn.

But before she made it to the great door, the deep, rich bass voice reached out like a warm hand to stop her. "Ivey?"

She glanced back to find that he wasn't brushing the mare anymore and instead was leaning one arm along the animal's haunches to look at her.

"You did some pretty fine growin' up. Welcome home," he said with a hint of a devilish smile.

"Thanks," she said quietly, wondering why such a small thing could send a secret little shock wave of delight through her.

Then she faced forward and went the rest of the way out, feeling his gaze on her backside as she did and only imagining that he might have that same mildly appreciative expression on his face as before.

But as she walked through the house again, locking it up, and then headed across to the other Heller property, it wasn't so much Cully's appearance or expressions that she carried with her. It was the idea he'd given her about staying here, for a little while anyway. And she was surprised to find herself seriously considering it.

Being in the old house hadn't been so terrible, and if she spent some time here she could tie up the loose ends still dangling after all these years. She could go through the things left in the house since their father's death. She could check out the ranch and give Savannah an informed opinion about whether or not they should sell the place.

Since she'd already taken a leave of absence from her teaching job, no one would miss her. It really might not be a bad idea for her to stick around.

Besides, the thought of seeing Cully Culhane every day was better than the thought of going back to Cheyenne and facing Arlen Earl Brunswell's wrath.

A whole lot better.

And maybe the next time she could manage not to bite his head off and actually have a conversation with him.

Funny, but that suddenly seemed like a good goal.

And almost enough reason all by itself to stick around.

Chapter Two

Cully Culhane woke up with one thing on his mind the next morning. The same thing that had been on his mind since it had happened—meeting up with Ivey Heller the day before.

He didn't understand why that was something to be replaying itself in his mind for the last twenty-four hours. Almost without a break, since he'd even dreamed about her. But there it was.

The sun wasn't up yet but that dream had brought him out of sleep to stare up at the dark ceiling above him, wondering about himself, about the lingering effects of what couldn't have been more than ten minutes with Linc and Jackson's cousin.

Ivey Heller.

His memory of her from fifteen years ago was pretty general. Which in itself was a sign of how she'd changed, because if she'd looked the way she did now, he definitely would have taken more notice. Those were the days when a female face and body were the only things he'd thought were important. Before he'd learned the hard way that a terrific face and body didn't necessarily make for a terrific woman.

What he did recall of Ivey was that she'd been a gangly and awkward young girl. Not pretty by any stretch of the imagination. And so tomboyish that sometimes when he'd passed her father's property and seen her outside, he'd thought she was a boy from the distance.

No mistaking her for a boy now.

Maturity had done remarkable things for her. The woman he'd met up with yesterday was more than pretty. She was beautiful. And feminine. And filled out to perfection.

No, she didn't look anything like he remembered. Except maybe for her hair. It was still that reddish blond color, still curly, only now she seemed to know what to do with it. Now it wasn't just a frizzy bowl-cut on top of her head the way it had been before. It was much longer, falling around her shoulders, looking soft and touchable.

One thing he hadn't remembered at all was the color of her eyes. As purple as spring violets. And with the longest lashes he'd ever seen.

But so what? he demanded of himself as he jammed his hands behind his head and pushed away the mental image of her standing in that barn.

So what if she had skin so smooth it seemed air-brushed? Or a cute turned-up nose? Or lips like peaches and cream?

So what if she had a tight little fanny his hands had

wanted to cup? Or breasts that just barely peeked out at him from behind that T-shirt she'd had on?

Were those any reason to have her on his mind all this time?

Hell, there were women all over the place. In town. Around town. Beautiful women. Nice women. Available women. But not a one of them had taken up residence in his head like Ivey Heller had.

Not a one of them since Kim.

And that's how he wanted it.

Didn't he have his hands full enough? What did he need with thoughts of some violet-eyed woman who was supposed to have been getting married this weekend?

He needed her barn. He needed her land—that was why he and his brothers were looking to buy her out. But he didn't need to be remembering the way she looked. He didn't need to be hearing her voice over and over, soft, sweet—at least it had been until he'd aggravated her. He sure didn't need to be watching her walk away a hundred times over in his mind so he could get another mental look at her backside...

Damned if he wasn't doing it again—letting his mind wander on its own.

Well, he wasn't going to stand for it, by God. He could control it.

And to prove it, he concentrated on the day ahead of him.

As always it was a full one since he, Yance and Clint ran the whole ranch without much hired help. Harvest season was coming to a close. Most of the hay was baled but it all still needed to be brought in from the fields and stacked for winter. And then there were the girls—

As if his thinking about them was their cue to come in, his bedroom door opened and in walked two tiny, pajama-clad waifs who climbed onto either side of his bed and curled up next to him.

"Mornin' girls," he said.

"Mornin'," Amy answered.

"I'm s'irsty for some juice," Randa contributed.

Cully pulled his hands out from under his head and wrapped an arm around each of his daughters. "What'd I tell you about staying in your beds?" he said, just to remind them about a rule he was trying to put into effect so that on the days he could sleep in till six or so, they didn't come and wake him at five anyway.

"I dunno, what'd you tell'd us?" Randa asked innocently. She was the younger of his girls, at three.

"I said you had to stay in your beds until you can see some light outside."

"But who's gonna turn on the light outside if everybody's sleepin'?" Amy reasoned. She was four.

"Not that kind of light. Light from the daytime starting up. I explained that to you." He knew enough after three years on his own with these two that they took everything literally. If he said they couldn't get up until they saw sunshine they wouldn't know what to do on a cloudy day. Or at least that's what they'd tell him as an excuse for why they wouldn't wait for daybreak the next half-dozen mornings after a cloudy day kept them waiting for the sun.

He also knew he should send them back to their room now, to stand firm on his rule, but there they were, two warm, cuddly little bundles nuzzled against him and he didn't have the heart. Or the inclination.

"I'm still s'irsty," Randa confided in a whisper.

"An' I'm reee-ly hungry, too. I didn't get my cookies and milk last night, 'member?" Amy added.

"But I needs juice first."

"Nuh-uh, I needs some cereal first."

"Okay, okay, don't start," he interrupted before tiny-tot war broke out.

Yep, he had all he could handle, all right, between raising these two and working the ranch. All he *wanted* to handle. And he was sticking to his vow to keep his distance from any kind of relationship with a woman. The vow he'd made after his divorce. No matter how many times Ivey Heller popped into his mind.

He'd just like it better if she didn't. If he had a little more luck keeping her out of it.

"*Now,* Daddy," Randa insisted with a bit of her temper in her tone.

And just like that, Cully couldn't help thinking about a similar tone in Ivey Heller's voice the day before. She hadn't wanted to talk about that wedding that hadn't happened.

Why hadn't it happened? he wondered.

And why was she so touchy about it?

Her cheeks had turned as pink as cotton candy and she'd gotten all riled and uppity...

Just what he needed, he reminded himself, a woman who got all riled and uppity. Who was probably as cantankerous as her old man had been.

Get the hell out of my head, will you? he thought as if the images in his mind were real and he could order them away. *My hands are full enough without you comin' 'round botherin' me.*

Damn it all to hell, what had gotten into him?

He didn't have an answer to that. But if he couldn't lie in bed and stop thinking about her, maybe he could stop thinking about her if he got up, got busy, got to work.

"Okay, girls, let's go," he said.

But even as he gave in to his daughters and swung out of bed, Ivey Heller lingered on the edges of his thoughts as if taunting him, daring him not to think about her.

And for one of the rare times in his life, he wasn't sure it was a dare he could take and make good on.

Ivey didn't sleep much later on her second morning in Elk Creek than she had on her first. But it was the chore she'd set for herself that roused her today.

She may have ceded to her sister's judgment that the wedding itself was not a time to confront Arlen, but she felt as if she needed to now. Leaving him at the altar had been a crummy thing to do and the least she owed him was an apology.

She knew his schedule well. Knew when he got up every morning. What he did. What the best time was to catch him before he left for the bank. What the best time was to catch him once he was there.

And she didn't doubt that he would be either there or getting ready to go there, rather than taking the time off he'd planned for their honeymoon. If there was one thing she knew about Arlen, it was that he loved his bank and his position as head of it. He hadn't really even wanted to go on a honeymoon since it meant a full week away. So, as things had turned out, Ivey was reasonably sure he'd just go on with work as usual.

Her plan had been to make the call in that slot before work, to talk to him at home. But just as she was about to do it she lost her nerve and discovered she was longing to shower and dress first. As if the clothes would be armor to protect her against her ex-fiancé's wrath.

That was what she ended up doing, fleeing into the warm spray of the water, then opting for a navy blue knit jumpsuit cut like a flight suit, which she always felt comfortable in.

Then she spent a few minutes bending over to scrunch her damp hair into maximum curls so she could leave it hanging loose around her shoulders—the way it looked best, but also the way she liked it most. Even though Arlen wouldn't be able to see her efforts, she was aiming for a boost to her confidence. She wanted to feel in top form to face this.

She still had a few minutes before she'd be able to get Arlen at his office, so she made the bed, straightened the room and then opened the curtains to the early morning autumn sunshine.

The last of those curtains covered a window that looked out on the front yard and the drive up to the house. When she realized that she paused.

She'd lost her sense of just how spread out everything was here. From the second-story window she could barely see a hint of her own house in the distance.

There was no way she could see anything of the Culhanes' place because it was more than three miles down the road.

But for some reason she kept standing at that window, trying to. And wondering as she did if Cully was there at that moment. Or if he was out on the range. Or in her barn, maybe...

Not that it made any difference. She didn't even know why it had occurred to her. Except maybe that she was distracting herself rather than thinking about the conversation to come with Arlen. Thinking about anything was preferable to that.

But what was her excuse for having thought so much about Cully the rest of the time since seeing him yesterday? she asked herself.

She didn't have an answer.

And she *had* thought a lot about Cully Culhane. More about him than about what she was going to say to Arlen—one more thing for which she felt terribly guilty.

Why was her former neighbor so stubbornly implanted in her brain?

Sure, he was terrifically handsome. So terrifically handsome that looking at him was like standing before a work of art. But she hardly knew the man and she was barely two days away from fleeing the scene of what was to be her wedding to another man. This was certainly not the time to be daydreaming about someone else.

But she had been daydreaming. Rewriting their meeting so it hadn't gotten them off on the wrong foot. Flirting with him in her mind. Drawing more of that assessing gaze of his that ended up giving her his seal of approval. Hearing over and over again that parting compliment on how well she'd grown up...

It was just so silly, she told herself. Not something a grown woman should be doing at all, let alone now, under the circumstances.

So cut it out!

She checked the clock on the nightstand beside the bed and realized her second window of opportunity to reach Arlen was upon her.

She took a deep breath and crossed the room, sitting

on the edge of the mattress and taking the desk phone into her lap.

But with one hand on the receiver, she hesitated.

Lord, what a mess she'd gotten herself into.

How could she even be entertaining romantic fantasies when she'd just botched one relationship so royally? When she'd just realized how awful and untrustworthy was her judgment of men? When she'd just recognized that she must have some commitment problems of her own?

She shouldn't be, that was all there was to it. She shouldn't even be thinking about Cully Culhane. She had no business doing it, she didn't want to do it, and she wasn't going to do it.

And to pay for the last full day and night of thoughts of him?

She picked up the receiver and dialed Arlen's office number in Cheyenne.

Part of the reason this particular time was opportune was that it was before Arlen's secretary came in to work. Ivey was not on good terms with her, in spite of having tried to make friends with her. She thought the secretary had rejected her overtures because the other woman harbored hopes of snagging Arlen for herself and didn't want any kind of pleasant acquaintance with the fiancée she was trying to depose.

Now Ivey hoped that really was the reason, hoped the secretary would offer Arlen some comfort. If he needed it.

But regardless of what the secretary did or did not have up her sleeve, it was bad enough to have to talk to Arlen now, without having to go through the other woman.

Ivey's timing was right because on the second ring he answered the phone himself.

She froze and couldn't get so much as a hello out until he'd repeated his impatient greeting from the other end.

"Arlen? It's me," she finally managed to say in a quiet voice.

Silence.

Ivey knew he was simmering. Building steam. Controlling it until he found just the right moment to release it and burn her.

"I wanted to call and apologize," she added.

"Apologize?" he said facetiously.

"I know it's pretty feeble after—"

"Feeble? Oh, yes, it's feeble all right. Tens of thousands of dollars for that wedding. Every person I know sitting there watching. And you send your sister to tell me you've already left the church and aren't going through with marrying me."

It didn't seem important to say that had been at Savannah's insistence. "I know it must have been awful for you. Embarrassing—"

"Try humiliating. Degrading—"

"I'm sorry. It was a terrible thing to do."

"Do you want to tell me *why* you did it?"

It also didn't seem fair to go into all the faults she'd found in him at the last minute. She was to blame for not having realized sooner that there were things about him she couldn't accept in a husband. Much, much sooner. So instead she said, "I had a change of heart."

"Oh, please."

"I just realized I didn't hear bells and whistles the way I thought I should." The moment the words came out of her mouth she knew it was a mistake to admit such a thing to the pragmatic Arlen.

Predictably, he seized on it. "*Bells and whistles?* Oh, for pity's sake. I know you're no more than a kindergarten teacher but that's just plain stupid. You sound like some airheaded teenager."

"It's only a figure of speech, Arlen," she said patiently. "What I meant was that I realized I didn't feel about you the way I should have felt—*wanted* to feel—about the man I was going to marry. And I don't think you feel that way about me, either."

"Do I hear *bells and whistles* about you? No, I don't."

"Well, I think you should. I think that kind of special, powerful feeling is something we both deserve to have...for ourselves and from each other, too."

"Oh, please," he repeated, more snidely than before.

"I couldn't commit to a lifetime with you without—"

"*Bells and whistles.*"

"I'm sorry," she said yet again.

And then the steam blew.

She listened without comment as Arlen berated her, called her names, reacted exactly the way she'd expected him to. It all came out in anger instead of jokes, of course, but basically what he railed about involved the same put-downs and criticisms that had caused her to stop the wedding before it had gotten started.

"I don't know what else to say except that I apologize," she told him when he ran out of steam.

"Should that surprise me? That you don't know what else to say? Because it doesn't. If you had a brain you'd be dangerous."

She ignored that. "I'll leave you my half of the

money in our joint account to make up for some of
what you spent on the wedding. I know it won't reimburse you for all of your portion, but it's something.''

"Who's going to reimburse me for being a laugh-
ingstock? For what I have to face from everybody
while you're off hiding wherever it is you're hiding?''

"I'm not hiding. I'm at my cousin's ranch in Elk
Creek. Maybe, if things are bad for you there, you
should take the time off work that you were going to
for the honeymoon, go on a vacation.''

"And just blow off what I'm needed here for? I was
only doing that because of you, not because I wanted
to. Some of us have responsibilities. Some of us live
up to our commitments. But I don't suppose that's anything you could understand.''

"It wouldn't have been right to go through with the
wedding, Arlen.''

"Look who's lecturing me on right and wrong—
Miss Bells and Whistles. Save it for those little rug rats
you work with. Maybe they'll buy into your garbage.''

She hated when he called her kindergartners *rug rats*
and he knew it. But she didn't take issue with that,
either.

"I'll let you get back to work now,'' was her only
response. "Savannah said she'll take care of returning
all the early wedding gifts since they're on display in
our apartment. Will you see about any that were left at
the church?''

"I already have,'' he snarled.

Ivey waited for more of his tirade, feeling as if she
had an obligation to hear him out, to let him vent whatever he needed to.

But when no more came, she said, "I guess that's about all there is to say then. Take care of yourself."

"Right," he snapped before he slammed the phone down so hard the sound bounced against her eardrum.

She replaced the receiver in the cradle and set the phone back on the nightstand, feeling a fresh wave of guilt even as she did.

But then, all at once, the image of Cully popped into her mind and just that fast she found herself feeling better. Lighter. Happier. For no reason she could fathom.

Yet there it all was and at that particular moment, she was too grateful for the reprieve to fight it.

Besides, it didn't mean anything, she told herself. Thoughts of Cully Culhane were just an escape valve.

An escape valve she wouldn't need anymore now that the worst of owning up to what she'd done was behind her.

This was probably the last time she'd even think about him.

And that would suit her just fine.

Or at least that's what she told herself.

Ivey spent the morning arranging for a plumber, an electrician, and someone from the phone company to meet her at her old family home that afternoon. After fifteen years of the house's being unoccupied, she wanted to make sure the flip of a switch wouldn't burn the place down, or the flush of a toilet flood it with sludge. And, of course, she had to have a phone.

Her cousins thought she was crazy to go to all the trouble if she wasn't moving in permanently—which she wasn't—and each one had assured her she was welcome to stay with them for as long as she wanted. But she didn't like being an imposition. Besides, the prospect of whipping the old house into shape appealed to her. It would give her something to do.

After getting herself all done up to make the phone call to Arlen, she wasn't dressed for work, so she decided to just get rid of the sheets that covered the furniture while she waited for the workmen to do their jobs through the afternoon.

She folded all the sheets in upon themselves and took them into the mudroom, where she made a pile, intent on shaking them out and washing them later.

With each trip into that small room that also held an old washing machine and dryer, she couldn't help glancing out the back door toward the barn.

Okay, so she was keeping an eye out for Cully.

She couldn't seem to stop picturing in her mind the way they'd met the day before, glancing out that tattered screen and seeing him walk into the barn on long cowboy-booted strides, a big, muscular brick wall of a man.

And she kept expecting to see it all over again every time she directed her gaze there.

What would she do if she did see him? she asked herself. Would she go out again? What would she say?

Whole scenarios developed in her mind, played themselves out, and before she knew it it was five o'clock. The power was on in the house. The wiring, outlets and electrical appliances had all been given the green light. The drains and commodes had been snaked out and were in working order. The furnace had been cleaned, primed and turned on and so had the telephone. The septic tank had been checked, as had the well, which was judged bacteria free. And all without Ivey doing much more than daydreaming.

About the only thing she had accomplished beyond getting rid of the dustcovers was a realistic appraisal of the rest of the work that needed to be done.

The walls would have to be washed; the hardwood floors polished; the rugs and mattresses taken out, beaten and aired; the furniture all vacuumed and the bathrooms and kitchen scrubbed down. Not to mention the minor structural repairs that were needed both inside and out.

It was a big job and one she realized she would need to hire help with, the same way she'd needed to hire help for what had been done today.

Not that she couldn't ask her cousins for that help, because she could. And they'd give it without complaint. But they were busy with their own work, their own lives, and she didn't feel right infringing on them more than she already had. So hiring help seemed like the best solution.

And once again her thoughts turned to Cully.

Just about the same time she finally spotted him riding in on horseback from across the open field that connected their two properties.

She stepped out the back door onto the small stoop so he'd see her and she wouldn't have to come up on him from behind and startle him again.

It also allowed her a better look at him, though she didn't admit that even to herself.

Dressed the way he had been the morning before in cowboy boots, jeans and a Western shirt—this one was red—he also wore a Stetson hat low on his brow.

He looked as if he'd had a tough day because soil and salt stains marked both his hat and his shirt and he seemed in no hurry to get where he was going.

Ivey waved—just in case he might not notice her—

and received a bare raising of his chin in acknowledgment before he reined in the horse at the fence of the paddock next to the barn.

His dismount was slow, too, but graceful nevertheless as one long leg swung over the horse and he stepped down. While he tied the reins to the fence's top rail, Ivey headed in his direction.

It seemed as if the closer she got to him, the faster her heart beat, but she wrote it off to nerves. After all, her friendly overture the morning before had turned sour, so it was only natural to be uneasy about approaching Cully again.

Then, too, it didn't help that his back was to her and her eyes drifted down the straight line of his spine to his waist where it narrowed and turned into a to-die-for derriere.

It was good when he'd finished tying the reins and turned around to face her.

Or at least that was what she pretended, to get rid of the regret that washed through her when she could no longer look at his backside.

He removed his hat just as she drew up in front of him, reached around to set it on the saddle's pommel and shook his head like a dog shakes off water. Then he raked his hands through his hair, more a gesture of shedding the effects of having worn the hat for a long time than anything that resembled vanity. And it didn't change the fact that his sable-colored hair bore a distinctive hat ring.

Not that it mattered. He was still great-looking, and in fact, there was a very masculine sensuality to his movements that for some reason sent a flash through her mind that imagined that same finger-combing when he stepped from a shower, his big body bare and glistening...

Ivey mentally kicked herself and forced her gaze upward to his face.

It didn't help the feelings that were tiptoeing through her when that gaze settled on the five o'clock shadow of his beard and discovered it added an appealing ruggedness to his appearance.

"I wondered if you'd be here tonight," she said by way of greeting.

"Mornings and evenings. Animals have to be seen to," he answered.

She couldn't distinguish any particular attitude to his tone so didn't know if he bore a grudge for the day before or not. She decided it was best to address it, though, and get it over with.

"I'm sorry for biting your head off yesterday. I guess I'm a little testy when it comes to the wedding. I hope you won't take it personally."

He did a scant shrug of one broad shoulder. "No harm done."

"I'm glad." *Too* glad. Being so near to him was not only keeping her pulse rate up but now it was making her feel as if she had butterflies in her stomach. "So are we okay, you and I?"

His lips stretched into a lazy smile and his incredible ice blue eyes seemed to take a quick—but thorough—survey of her from top to bottom. "I know I am. And you don't look any the worse for wear," he said with a full helping of the charm that had made him so popular with the girls in school.

Ivey felt her cheeks flush the way they had the previous morning but she forged on, hoping a business discussion would distract from it. "Then I wondered if

I might be able to hire you." Why had that sounded a tad flirtatious? It made her want to bite her tongue. Instead she added in a hurry, "To help me with some work around here. There's some handyman kinds of things that need to be done to the house, and I need someone with some muscle to drag out rugs and mattresses and beat the dust out of them."

The words still came out sounding almost intimate and for the life of her, Ivey didn't know what had gotten into her.

Cully's lazy smile stayed in place. "So you decided to stay, did you?"

"Not forever. But for a while. Long enough to need the house spruced up to live in it."

He nodded, watching her with that penetrating gaze. "No job to go back to?"

"I teach kindergarten, but I took a leave of absence for this semester so I'm not due back until January." It came as a surprise to her to realize that after so many put-downs of her work by Arlen she was embarrassed to say what she did.

But Cully's response was far from a put-down. His thick brows arched. "A schoolteacher," he repeated. "Are you good at it?"

She thought about that, discovering more damage Arlen had done because she had to consider her answer before she could say, "I think I am good at it, yes. My reviews are always high and my kids seem to like me, so I must be." And it was a pleasant change to feel proud of it in a way she hadn't in a long time now.

"*Your* kids? As in students, or do you have some of your own?"

"As in students. I don't have any of my own."

"But you must like kids."

"Oh, sure. A lot. That's why I became a teacher in the first place."

He nodded that handsome head of his as if she'd given the right answer on a test. And for a moment she lost herself in the depths of that ice blue gaze.

"How come you can take so much time off without risking your job?" he asked then.

"I've been at the same school since I graduated college. And I rarely take a sick day or a personal one, so after this many years I had a lot of time coming." Still, she wasn't altogether comfortable talking about her work so she seized the fact that he hadn't answered her question about helping with the house and went back to it.

"So, anyway," she said. "I'm sure you're busy but do you think you could spare a day to work around here? I'll pay whatever you want..." Oh, great, the suggestive tone again. Where was it coming from?

The lazy smile returned to his lips—good lips, just full enough, with a slightly ironic upturn at the corners as if he didn't take anything too seriously.

"You may have forgotten since you've been away so long, but around here we don't have to be paid to help out a neighbor."

"It wouldn't be fair for me not to pay you. I really need a full day of your time so you'll be neglecting your own work."

"I don't think my bosses'll fire me for it or dock my pay," he said with a slight chuckle that rumbled from deep inside that big chest.

"Still, I'd feel better if I could compensate you."

This time she knew he heard the unintentionally insinuative note that kept lurking around the edges of her voice because his smile broadened and turned a touch mischievous. He couldn't seem to resist flirting back, although much more adeptly. "Did you have somethin' besides money in mind?"

She wanted to crawl into a hole, that's what she had in mind.

Or watch him do that hair combing with his hands again so she could relive her stepping-out-of-the-shower fantasy....

I've gone crazy, she thought. *Completely out of my mind.*

But what she said was, "A day's pay for a day's work," as if she were a teamster.

Somehow she knew he saw her discomfort, that he was aware that whatever this had sounded like was not what she'd meant for it to. And he seemed to be enjoying it, if his grin was any indication.

Of course he was no doubt used to women coming on to him—even if that wasn't what she was doing. And hey, after Arlen, she should be used to feeling like an idiot. But she wasn't. Especially when all this man had done to inspire it was get off his horse, remove his hat, finger-comb his hair and stand there reeking masculinity.

Maybe she'd heard Arlen tell her she was a fool so many times she'd turned into one.

Then, all of a sudden, Cully seemed to decide to give her a break and not rub it in anymore. "I'll tell you what," he said in a slightly—only slightly—more businesslike tone. "I'll make a deal with you instead of taking wages."

"Great. What kind of deal?"

"I'll help you, if you'll help me."

Maybe he wasn't giving her a break after all. "How

can I help you?'' she asked as cautiously as if she were walking through hot coals.

"I need to saddle break a horse I'm keeping over here and I can use somebody to watch my girls while I do."

The first thing that flashed through her mind was an image of his *girls* as a harem of scantily clad, buxom women. But surely he didn't need her to watch them.

"Your girls?'' she asked for clarification.

"My daughters. There's two of them. One three and one four.''

Kids. He had kids. And no doubt a wife to go with them.

Ivey's heart sank to her toes and that was when she knew she really must have gone around the bend. Why should that fact disappoint her? And so severely…

"Mom works?'' she guessed, saying it just the way she would to the dad of one of her students and thanking the Fates for finally granting her some control over her own voice.

"Their mother's long gone,'' he answered. "That's why I need somebody to watch them.''

Ivey's heart floated back up, higher, lighter than it had been before. "I'm sorry,'' she lied, even though she had no idea if being long gone meant the woman was deceased or just absent.

But he apparently didn't want to talk about it, because all he said to that was, "So what do you say? I'll give you tomorrow to work around here if you'll give me the next day of baby-sittin'.''

"Sure. That's more than a fair trade,'' she agreed without needing to think about it. In truth the prospect of meeting his children, seeing what he'd produced in the way of offspring, appealed to her too much to seem like repayment of any kind.

"It's a deal then. How early do you want me here?"

Who said she wanted him to leave?

But of course that thought was just another of those uncontrollable flashes she seemed prone to the last two days.

She finally decided it must be some odd side effect of the stress she'd been under with wedding preparations and ultimately realizing Arlen was not the man for her. She just hoped it would stop soon.

"There's a lot to do," she managed to say in answer to his question about a starting time for work the next day. "Would seven-thirty be too early?"

"That's fine."

"Will you be bringing your daughters? I mean, it's okay if you do."

"They'd be underfoot and we'd never get anything done. Besides, they have a play group most of the day—I was going to use the time to break the horse. Now I'll just do it the next day."

"Is that all right?"

"Sure. No big deal."

Silence fell again but he was looking at her very intently, studying her almost, as if waiting for more from her.

But there wasn't anything more to say. At least nothing she could think of. Unfortunately.

"Well then, I guess we're all set," she said.

"Guess we are," he agreed, still watching her with those luminous eyes that suddenly seemed to see right through her.

"I'll bring something for lunch," she said, to fill the third silence that fell.

"Fine."

"Are you finicky or allergic or something?"

"No, I'm easy," he said, the innuendo in his voice again, teasing her.

"All right then…"

He chuckled once more, his eyes still on her, as if he found her amusing for some reason. Then he said, "Are you always this nervous or do I just bring out the best in you?"

That didn't help.

"It's been a rough few days. I suppose I'm on edge."

He nodded as if he understood. "Well, let's see if we can't put your house in order and then maybe you'll feel better."

It was a nice thing to say, surprising her when she'd half expected him to have a bit of fun at her expense the way he might have as an ornery teenager. It made Ivey feel off the hook, helping her to relax some already.

"That would be good," she agreed before adding, "Tomorrow then."

Yet having said that as a goodbye she felt unaccountably reluctant to end even this second uneasy meeting with him and stayed standing there.

"Tomorrow. Seven-thirty. I'll be here," he confirmed as if he thought that was the reason she was still hanging around.

"Great. Have a nice night," she said as she finally turned to go, wishing she'd thought of something that didn't make her sound like a grocery store cashier.

"You have a nice night, too," he countered with another of those chuckles.

For the second time Ivey thought she could feel his

gaze on her as she walked away. But this time she couldn't imagine that it was appreciative.

She could only be grateful that he wasn't laughing at her for reverting to a silly schoolgirl and behaving as if he were an upperclassman she had a crush on.

Tomorrow she'd do better, she promised herself.

And the idea that she had another chance at it in the form of a definite appointment to see him again made up for just about everything.

Chapter Three

By seven o'clock the next morning Ivey was up, showered, dressed in jeans and a bright yellow sweatshirt, with her hair caught at her crown in an elastic ruffle and left in a curly topknot.

She spent until about five after seven applying a dab of foundation to her nose in an unsuccessful attempt to hide her freckles, a touch of mascara to highlight her eyes, and a little blush to accentuate her cheekbones.

Then, after making the bed and straightening the room, she muttered, "Sorry, Savannah, that's as long as I can wait to call," and dialed the number to the apartment in Cheyenne that she shared with her sister.

Savannah answered with a groggy hello.

"It's just me," Ivey informed her. "Rise and shine."

"I rose at 6:45. It will take at least another hour before I shine. But don't you sound chipper."

No surprise there. Ivey felt chipper. She just didn't want to attribute her good mood to the fact that she'd be seeing Cully in less than half an hour.

"I wanted to let you know what's going on," she said rather than address her sister's comment.

"Let me guess—you talked to Arlen," Savannah said, sounding suddenly much more awake.

"Yesterday. How did you know?"

"He was calling about every hour on the hour and pulled two surprise visits since the wedding because he was sure you were here. When it all stopped I thought he'd probably connected with you somehow."

"I'm sorry you had to take the brunt of it all. But thanks for not letting him know where I was so I could deal with him in my own good time."

"Does he know where you are now?"

"Yes. I told him when I called him."

"And what else did you tell him?"

"Not a lot. I apologized and explained. Sort of."

"And how not nice was he about it?"

Ivey chuckled at her sister's knowledge of Arlen and said with understatement, "He voiced his displeasure thoroughly."

"Big tongue-lashing," Savannah guessed.

"The biggest."

"Did he threaten to sue you?"

"Sue me? No, why?"

"That was what he said in my last conversation with him. He was going to sue you for breach of promise and me for aiding and abetting because I wouldn't tell him where you were. He was pretty wild at that point."

"Can't blame him for being upset."

Savannah didn't say anything to that. But then Ivey knew her sister's opinion of Arlen had changed over the last few months. At the same rate Arlen himself had changed, from what had seemed like a nice guy to the snide, put-down king he'd become.

"So, how are you doing?" Savannah asked.

"Fine. Good, as a matter of fact. I feel like a weight has been lifted off my shoulders." Which could also account for her being chipper so it didn't have to have anything to do with Cully.

"Are you coming home?"

"Not right away. That was part of what I wanted to tell you. I'm going to stay here for a while."

"In Elk Creek?" Savannah said as if Ivey might have moved and *here* meant somewhere else.

"It's kind of good to be back."

Savannah seemed to think about that. Then she said, "I don't suppose that's so far-fetched. Elk Creek always was a nice little town. It was just that it was where Dad was."

Neither of them added that now that their father was gone, the small town's only negative factor had been removed. But it was there between them anyway, as surely as if the sentiment had been voiced.

Ivey decided to put a more positive spin to it. "I like the idea of catching up with Linc and Jackson and Beth, and seeing old friends after so long. You ought to come, too."

"I don't think our cousins need more than one houseguest."

"That's no problem. I'm going to be opening up our place."

"You're kidding? After all this time? It must be a mess."

"It is. But when I decided to do this I had the plumbing and the wiring checked out and I'm on my way there today to clean it up and get it into livable shape.''

"Are you telling me you're moving in there for good?" Savannah asked very seriously and with no small amount of concern in her voice.

"No, not for good. But for a while. You know I don't have to be back in school until January and for some reason this just feels like the right place to regroup."

"Okay," her sister said, but dubiously. "You know you'll have to come back and face Arlen sooner or later."

"It isn't because of Arlen. I may very well never see him again no matter where I am. He knows it's over between us. I just thought that since I have some empty time on my hands I might as well finally go through the stuff here that we never went through after Dad died, check out whether or not we should sell to the Culhanes, things like that."

"The Culhanes. With so much going on I forgot Jackson said they want to buy the ranch."

"Well, they do and if we sell to them we'll need to know if there's anything from the house we want to keep. Plus it should be in decent shape for them."

"All three of them?" Savannah fished, her curiosity clearly roused.

"To tell you the truth, I don't know. I guess I just assumed the three of them are still here. But I've only seen Cully."

"Cully. The youngest of the three. Is he still as cute as he was?"

"Cuter."

There must have been something more than conversational in her tone because it seemed to set off an alarm in her sister. "Oh, no, Ivey, you haven't got a thing for him *already,* have you?"

"Don't be silly."

"That isn't why you decided to stay, is it?"

"No." Okay, so maybe it had influenced her. But only in a very, very tiny way, she was sure.

"Because you know rebound relationships are a mistake."

"*Any* relationship would be a mistake for me right now."

"But you noticed how cute Cully Culhane is," Savannah said ominously.

"I'd have to be blind not to notice that. It doesn't mean anything."

"Are you sure there's not a correlation between how cute he is and how *happy* you are?"

"I'm not dumb enough to get involved with anyone right now," Ivey said forcefully rather than answer her sister's question.

"Is he married?" Savannah asked hopefully, as if asking a high-wire walker if she was working with a net.

"No. But he does have two kids. Girls."

"Where's the wife?"

"Gone. That's all he'd say."

"Who did he marry? Anyone we know?"

"I don't know that either. See how aboveboard everything is? We haven't gotten into anything personal so you don't have to worry about me."

"But the Culhanes..."

"They're just people, Savannah. Not secret weapons."

"You may think that because you managed to avoid

the crush on them that most of the rest of us had, but now that you're grown-up and vulnerable…''

Vulnerable. She was vulnerable, Ivey admitted to herself. Which could account for part of why she had such trouble getting Cully Culhane out of her thoughts.

Still, forewarned was forearmed.

"I'll be careful not to succumb to his charms, Savannah. I promise," Ivey said as though she were already immune. Which she wasn't. Not by a long shot and she knew it.

"I don't know. The Culhanes were pretty irresistible."

"To wide-eyed girls. I'm a long way from that." Ivey glanced at the clock and realized she had just enough time to walk across the road to meet Cully at seven-thirty.

"I better let you go," she said to her sister, deciding not to tell Savannah that Cully was spending the day helping her whip their old house into shape. Why worry her?

But she did say, "I expect to be staying at our place by tonight. I had a phone put in so I won't be too isolated. Better write the number down."

"Just a minute. Let me find a pen."

Only a few seconds passed before Savannah gave the go-ahead and Ivey read the telephone number from a paper on which she had it written.

Then Savannah said, "You're sure you're okay?"

"It would have been a mistake to go through with the wedding—it wasn't a mistake to call it off. Or to come here," she assured her sister.

"Unless you fall in with Cully Culhane on the rebound," Savannah cautioned.

"Would you stop with the Cully Culhane stuff?"

"Just be careful. Those Culhanes are too hot for any woman to handle."

Ivey assured her sister she'd be careful and they said their goodbyes.

But as she left her cousin's house a few minutes later and headed for the old homestead across the road, she couldn't help thinking about Savannah's comments about the Culhanes, about her own vulnerability.

She knew her sister was right. At least about Cully.

He was powerfully attractive.

And she was definitely susceptible to it.

But that didn't mean she was going to give in to the man's charms.

No, today she was determined to keep in mind that good-looking or not, he was just someone she'd hired to do a job. She didn't have to be overly friendly, just polite. And she certainly wasn't going to let any of that involuntary flirting happen. She was going to do her work, and he was going to do his, and that was all there was to it.

She'd just ignore the fast pace of her heart and the flutters in her stomach at the simple thought that every step she took down her cousin's drive brought her closer to seeing him again.

Cully was already at the house as Ivey approached it carrying a small cooler full of food in one hand and a bucket with cleaning supplies she'd borrowed in the other.

He was reattaching the front screen door so his backside was the first thing she saw.

What a way to start the day!

Her gaze did a slow roll up from his cowboy boots to tight, timeworn blue jeans that were stretched smooth across thighs the size of telephone poles and that rear end that couldn't have been more taut or more perfect if it had been carved especially to set women on fire.

Ivey indulged in the sight for as long as it took to reason with herself, reprimand herself, remind herself that this kind of awe and admiration was what had knocked her off-kilter and left her behaving in ways she didn't want to behave. Then she forced her gaze the rest of the way up his jean-jacketed torso to where his shiny sable brown hair eased down the nape of a thick, strong-looking neck.

"Good morning," she called from a fair distance so as not to sneak up on him again. And to yank her own thoughts to the business at hand.

He gave a few last pulses of a screwdriver to tighten a hinge before he turned to her. "Mornin'."

Underneath the jean jacket he had on a steel gray shirt that snapped down the front from all but a few inches below the collar where the crew neck of a white T-shirt showed beneath it. His sharp jaw and the planes of his cheeks were clean shaven and as Ivey stepped onto the porch and drew nearer, she caught a whiff of aftershave that smelled like a cool mountain night.

She liked the scent. A lot. In fact it went right to her head.

Or maybe Cully's smile contributed to that because it was warm, welcoming and appreciative as his gaze took her in from topknot to toe.

"You're early," she said without needing to check the time because she knew she wasn't a minute later than seven-thirty. Not when she'd been so anxious to get here that she'd very nearly jogged the whole way.

"Early enough so your front screen is fixed," he

countered, proving the point by opening and closing the door.

"Great. I like a man with initiative," she said, setting down the cooler and the bucket to take the key out of the mailbox.

Cully opened the screen again and held it that way while she unlocked the old mahogany door.

She could see him reflected in the oval glass in the top half and had to fight a rush of the purest pleasure at just being there with him.

Be cool, she told herself in an attempt to slow the race of her pulse and counter the involuntary flirting that was threatening to creep into her voice again.

When she had the door open, she picked up the bucket again, but before she could reach for the cooler, Cully bent over and grabbed it.

Chivalrous, too. After Arlen that was a pleasant change of pace.

She led the way inside and as she headed for the kitchen she lifted the bucket slightly higher, nodding toward the thermos that was stuck in among the cleaning things.

"I brought coffee. Want a cup?"

"Maybe later," he said, following her into the house. "I'm bettin' we have so much work to do today we'd better not waste any time gettin' started."

That was true enough, even if it was a little disappointing not to have a few minutes with him over coffee.

"Why don't you lay out for me what needs to be done?" he suggested once they'd reached the kitchen.

That was a safe subject. It was hard to be even unwittingly flirtatious about dragging mattresses outside to beat fifteen years' worth of dust out of them, repairing the roof, renailing shutters, or washing windows from a ladder.

Ivey hoisted the bucket onto the countertop and emptied the contents as she outlined what she had in mind for him to do while she'd be concentrating on cleaning the house itself.

When she'd finished both the list of chores and emptying the bucket, she turned to face him and caught him staring at her rear end. Only rather than being unnerved, the way she would have been in his shoes, he just slid his gaze to her face and smiled a half smile that left her wondering if he'd seen her reflection in the front door's window when she'd come up on him earlier, knew she'd been ogling him and was just paying her back.

"I think I can handle all that," he said as if nothing but the work ahead of him was on his mind. But there was something in the way those ice blue eyes rested even on her face that said that wasn't the case, that he just might be as aware of her as she was of him.

It was unnerving. Yet it still sent a small thrill through her that she had to fight to ignore.

"What do you want me to use to beat the mattresses?" he asked her with a hint of teasing insinuation lurking around the edges of his voice.

The man still had the streak of mischief that the boy had been known for, she realized. And he probably thought she was an easy target.

But not today she wasn't. She was determined to stay on the straight and narrow with him, so she pretended not to notice and stuck strictly to business.

"I was thinking you might use my old baseball bat. I'm sure it's still up in the closet in my room."

"That ought to work. Why don't I start with the

mattresses then, so they can sit out in the fresh air and sun most of the day before I put them back?''

"Good idea. Can you bring them down by yourself or will it take both of us?''

"I think I can manage. Why don't you get going with your work and I'll call you if I need help.''

"Okay.''

That hadn't gone too badly, Ivey thought as Cully set the cooler on the table and left the kitchen to climb the stairs. She'd managed a normal exchange with him and for the first time didn't feel as if she'd made a fool of herself.

It gave her some hope that she really could keep her wits about her if she set her mind to it.

This whole thing would be fine, she thought. After all, working with Cully was no different than working with Linc or Jackson, so why shouldn't they be able to just get the job done and be none the worse for wear?

Still, she didn't budge from the spot she'd been in when he'd left the room. A part of her held on to the hope of hearing his deep voice asking for her help.

But it never came because he didn't need it. He slid all three of the double-size mattresses down the steps and out the front door without any problems, and then went back for the baseball bat that was right where she'd said it would be.

An even rhythm of thuds told her he'd gotten right to work after that last trip up and down the stairs and Ivey almost slipped into the living room to watch him. But she resisted the urge. She was tougher than that.

And to prove it, she went to work herself, vowing to immerse herself in her cleaning chores and not even think about him. She started with the kitchen since that's where she was—and since it was on the opposite side of the house from where Cully happened to be.

But as hard as she worked scrubbing out cupboards, washing dishes, appliances, walls and floors, it took equally as much effort to keep that vow.

It was just plain impossible to be completely oblivious to the man.

Especially when she could see him at every turn, and when, as if he were in some tantalizing strip show, he removed one article of clothing after another to accommodate the rising temperature of the autumn day.

First, about midmorning, went the jean jacket. Then he rolled the sleeves of his shirt up to his elbows, baring muscular forearms speckled with hair just red enough to gleam in the sunshine.

Then he took off the shirt altogether and worked only in the T-shirt that fit every bulging muscle of his chest, shoulders, back and biceps so closely it could have been whitewashed on.

If there was nothing else to be said for the tough, physical life on a ranch, it certainly made for a hard, honed, well-proportioned body. And Ivey was only human. She couldn't help noticing it each time Cully came into view as the morning wore on.

But even so, working with him and giving herself continuous reminders to treat him like one of her cousins, helped ease the tension Ivey had felt the other times she'd been with Cully. Plus there was something about being back in the old house that brought out that childhood tomboy in her. Not with any kind of strong force, but just enough to lend her a little courage, to take away some of her self-consciousness.

By the time noon rolled around she'd stopped worrying about reverting to any kind of smitten-teenager behavior and felt calm and in control enough to actually look forward to sitting down with Cully and having lunch. Just the two of them. Maybe getting him to catch her up on some of the people and events in Elk Creek.

But it wasn't to be.

Just as noon arrived, so did one of the ranch hands from her cousin's place.

It was her own fault. She'd asked Jackson if someone could bring over her suitcases at some point today. But the ranch hand also used the opportunity of being there to make a friendly request of Cully to show him a new horse out in the barn.

Cully ended up taking his lunch to eat along the way and Ivey was left on her own—and disappointed for the second time that day, even though she knew she shouldn't be. After all, Cully was just working for her. He didn't have any obligation to eat with her.

She spent the early portion of the afternoon cleaning the upstairs and then she and Cully both got started on the window washing.

Cully finished ahead of Ivey because he could hose off the outsides initially, then use a rag and window cleaner to make them glisten, while Ivey could only employ elbow grease to get the job done on the inside.

So she was still working at it when he moved on to pounding the shutters back into place.

Standing at the windows the way she was, she couldn't help catching even more glimpses of him and, try as she might, she couldn't keep from appreciating the sight. In fact, every look at him sent the oddest little undertone of excitement rippling through her.

Only this time she didn't feel bad or embarrassed about all the glances in Cully's direction because he was casting a few of his own at her.

Enough of them so that at the end of the afternoon when they were both working on the same upstairs bedroom window from their opposite perches he missed the nail he was aiming at and hit his thumb with the hammer instead.

"Ow! Dammit!"

Ivey slid the window upward to open it, leaned slightly out of it and let the tomboy in her taunt him as if he really were Linc or Jackson. "I thought you were better with a hammer than that, Culhane. Are you all right?"

He chuckled, shook the pain out of his hand and said, "I think I'll live, *Heller.*"

"Want to suck on it and make it better? I won't tell anybody about it if you do."

He looked at her through narrowed eyes and an ornery smile of his own. "I gave up sucking my own thumb a long time ago."

She ignored the innuendo in his voice and went on teasing him. "Want a bandage for your boo-boo then?"

"No, I don't want a *bandage* for my *boo-boo.*"

"Want me to kiss it and make it better?" Where had *that* come from? Certainly not from the tomboy in her! It might have been something she would have said to goad one of her cousins, but it hadn't come out sounding quite the same way it would have to one of them.

Cully laughed. "Who are you kidding? You'd drop dead on the spot if I said yes."

"Think so, huh?"

"I know so."

"Don't be too sure."

He thrust his hand toward her. "Okay, then do it," he challenged.

Ivey reared back, away from the big, callused hand with its long, thick fingers. "All right, all right, I was only bluffing."

"Too bad," he muttered with a half grin that said he'd known it the whole time.

He gave the nail one last tap before he said, "You want the screens up or do you think it's late enough in the year to leave 'em off?"

She could tell he was feeling relaxed with her, too. It came out in the more casual, amiable way he talked to her. Something else about him that she liked.

"I think we'll leave the screens off," she said.

"That makes me about finished out here then. You ready for me to bring in the mattresses?"

"The windows in this room are my last, too, so that'll work for me. And then I guess we'll be through for the day," she added, surprised to find just how sorry she was about that. "I'd offer you a beer for a job well-done but I don't have any," she said, thinking out loud of a way to keep him around a little longer.

"That's okay."

He didn't have any reason not to climb down from the ladder, but he didn't do it. Instead he leaned one arm on the head step and said, "You don't have anything to eat or drink in this whole place, do you?"

"Water. Or what's left of that coffee in the thermos. Want some?"

"No. I was just thinkin' about you stayin' here tonight. You don't have a way into town on your own, either, do you?"

"My car is still in Cheyenne," she confirmed.

They both knew she had her cousins right across the road to supply food or transportation, but neither of them said it.

What Cully did say was, "Tell you what, if you don't mind havin' my girls along, how about I buy you some supper in town tonight? You can call Kansas over at the store, have her bag up some groceries and leave 'em at Margie Wilson's café for you after the store closes up—I'm sure Kansas would let you settle the bill later on since you're her cousin-in-law—and that way you'll be able to stock your cupboard. I'd hate to see you starve over here," he added with a devilish smile to go with the trumped-up excuse that made her think he wasn't any more eager to have this day end than she was.

But as appealing as his offer was, Ivey told herself she should decline it. That no matter how much she worked to treat him the way she'd treat her cousins, the truth was she didn't think of him as anything remotely that benign.

Then she remembered that he'd said his kids would be along and that made a difference to her. A big difference.

Or maybe she was just looking for any old excuse....

Either way she heard herself say, "I'd appreciate a ride into town. On one condition, though."

"What's that?"

"I buy dinner. Call it a bonus for a job well-done today."

"No deal."

"But I want to treat."

He shot her a mock frown at the same time his lips curled up into a wry smile. "Are you confusin' me with some city fella who'd let a woman pay for his supper?"

"Country men don't stand for it?"

"Not one worth his salt. You ought to know that."

"How would I know that? I was just a kid when I lived here. The only dinners I had in restaurants were paid for by my family. I never had anything that could be called a date. Not that dinner tonight would be a date..." she added in a hurry because she wasn't sure exactly what dinner tonight would be.

His smile broadened, lifting higher on one side than the other. But he didn't clarify exactly what dinner tonight would be. He just said, "You never had a single date growin' up?"

"Not one."

"Not even to a school dance?"

"Not even a school dance."

"How'd we overlook you?"

"Pretty easily," she said with a laugh.

"Be hard to do now."

She felt heat rise in her cheeks but she raised her chin anyway. "Well, good. Who likes to be overlooked?"

His eyes met hers and held them with an expression that seemed to say he was enjoying this. Enjoying her. And it warmed her as much as his compliments did.

"So say you'll have dinner with me, Heller," he prompted.

"Okay, I'll have dinner with you. But I still want to pay."

He ignored that last part. "Then you'd best go in and call Kansas to catch her so she has time to do your shoppin' and get it over to the café."

He was right but Ivey didn't want to rush away. This was too nice.

Cully poked that sharp chin of his in the direction just past her and said, "Go on."

"Are you trying to get rid of me?"

"Thought I was tryin' to light a fire under you so we could get ourselves cleaned up and have our dinner."

"Ah," she said, silently agreeing that that was an even more appealing idea. "Sure you can get down from that ladder without hurting yourself if I'm not here?" she asked, just to give him a hard time and cover up how effective his charm was.

"I'll manage," he assured wryly.

Ivey reached up and slid the window closed between them, forcing herself not to stare at him the whole time.

But before she left that spot she stole a last glance and found him still leaning on one arm, not even attempting to camouflage his study of her.

And smiling just cockily enough to let her know he liked what he saw.

Would the dinner be a date? she wondered.

Not that it mattered.

She couldn't have been any more excited whether it was or not, because whatever anyone called it, it meant she got to see Cully more today after all.

Once Cully had left, Ivey showered and shampooed away the day's grime in the old house's sole bathroom—upstairs, across the hall from the bedroom she and Savannah had shared. The same bedroom she'd taken for herself now rather than use the larger one at the end of the hallway that had belonged to their father.

She'd made up both her old bed and her sister's because she hated looking at a bare mattress, but only closed the door on the other room. She was too short on time and energy to make that bed, too.

She really was bone weary, she thought when the shower made her body long for a comfortable chair to fall into and not budge out of until it was time to go to sleep for the night. But anticipation of the dinner—or actually of the company ahead—made her ignore it.

She put on a dark purple knit dress with a high turtleneck and long dolman sleeves that she pushed partway up her forearms. The bodice wasn't tight, but it draped her curves just right, and the full skirt went all the way to the middle of her calves—four inches over the smooth black leather boots she wore. Pointy-toed dress boots with two-inch heels, not cowboy boots.

She left her hair down in one wild cascade of curls and applied only a light touch of makeup, but she did it all as carefully as if she were primping for the prom. Which was also about how high her excitement level climbed the nearer it got to Cully's arrival time.

Ivey had just put the finishing touches on with a bare hint of pale lipstick when she heard his knock on the front door. She hurried down the stairs, taking a deep breath and reminding herself yet again not to get carried away by the attraction she felt for him and to treat him the same way she'd treat either of her cousins.

But then she opened the door and just about every resolution she'd ever made was like so much smoke in the wind as she drank in the sight of Cully.

He was dressed all in black—black cowboy boots, skintight black jeans, and a black Western shirt that hugged his flat stomach but still managed to widen all the way out to shoulders so broad they blocked her view of the moon in the distance. He even had on a black belt, although its big silver buckle broke up the dark color.

That buckle held her gaze for a split second longer than she should have spent looking in that direction but luckily when she yanked her eyes upward she found

Cully so intent on taking in her appearance that he hadn't realized what she'd been staring at.

"Well, don't you clean up just fine," he said, his tone making the words an understatement.

"So do you," she countered with a small laugh as she caught a fresh whiff of that aftershave she'd smelled in the morning and liked so much. Almost as much as she liked the vision of his newly shaved face and hair that was so clean it shined in the porch light she'd turned on earlier.

In an attempt to slow down the race of her blood she stopped looking at him and looked beyond him for signs of his daughters.

When she didn't see them on the porch or in the big white pickup truck that was parked in front of it, she said, "Where are your kids?"

"They wouldn't come. Seems my brothers promised them a night of popcorn and watching *The Little Mermaid* and they decided they'd rather do that. They're always doing this to me—they get a better offer and they throw me away like a dirty shirt," he joked and his half smile was enough to keep her blood racing no matter what she did.

She hadn't opened the screen door yet and rather than reaching for the knob to do it himself Cully braced one palm against the frame and leaned his weight against it.

"So we're fresh out of chaperons," he said then. "What do you think of that?"

She thought she should turn tail and run as fast as she could from a man who could evoke so much inside her with just his appearance, or a simple compliment, or a single charming smile.

But for the life of her, she couldn't do it.

"If I remember right, being in Elk Creek is like having a dozen chaperons. Everybody watches everybody else," she said.

"True enough. But there's still the drive to and from. That could be dangerous territory," he teased.

"I think it'll be okay. Pull anything funny and I'll sic my cousins on you," she joked in return, a threat she'd used a time or two as a child.

"That'll keep me on the straight and narrow all right. I can handle Linc and Jackson, but I understand Beth has one mean punch," he said with a laugh.

He pushed himself off the door frame and pulled the screen open. "Want to chance it, then?"

In answer Ivey grabbed the small shoulder bag she'd hung from the hall tree next to the door and flipped off the light in the entryway. "Okay, but watch yourself," she said in mock warning as she stepped outside into the cool autumn air.

"I'd rather watch you," he answered as he reached in and pulled the door closed behind her.

She pretended not to hear that because she didn't know what to say to it. But it warmed her just the same and she took a secret smile with her across the porch to the steps—the broken one fixed now and the rest reinforced, thanks to Cully.

They reached the truck at the same time and Cully opened that door for her, too, holding his hand out for her to help her climb in.

Ivey hesitated.

It was silly, she knew. It was just his hand and he was only offering a simple courtesy.

But it still meant they'd be touching. And she wasn't too sure what kind of effect that might have on her.

Yet she didn't know how to refuse without offending

him. Not to mention that a part of her was all in favor of that touching. So she gave in and took his hand.

Big, warm, callused. And charged. Or at least that was what flashed through her mind as his grasp set off little currents of electricity to dance along her nerve endings.

"Thanks," she muttered as she got into the cab and took her hand out of his as soon as possible to escape the sensation she liked much, much more than she should have.

He closed her door and rounded the truck bed. While he did Ivey took another deep breath, swore to herself that this was no different than being with Linc or Jackson, and hoped like crazy that she'd regained some small amount of composure by the time Cully got behind the wheel and started the engine.

Apparently he'd been playing the radio on his way over because it came on again automatically to fill the cab with the disc jockey's voice.

"I'm about to call it a night, folks, head home to my family and turn this station over to our taped music like always. But before I do I have one last announcement that just came in. Seems the Hellers are gettin' together a barbecue out at Jackson's place tomorrow night so we can all have a chance to say hey to their cousin Ivey—"

Ivey laughed at that. Jackson had called her not half an hour before to ask what she thought of the idea and now here it was on the radio.

"This here is an invitation to anybody who'd like to come on out for some food and libation. I know me and mine'll be there. We're all glad to have Ivey back home again. Maybe we can even talk her into stayin'. Elk Creek loses too many fillies to the city. Be nice to

*lure her home for good. So anyway, anytime long about
sundown, Jackson'll be firin' up the barbecue and I
hear his new wife Ally'll be makin' some of her spe-
cialties from her time as a Denver chef. Hope to see
you all out there. And Ivey, if you're listenin', welcome
home.''*

Cully flipped the radio off as the disc jockey went
into his sign-off.

"Bucky Dennehy," Ivey said, recognizing the voice
that had come over the airwaves.

"Yep."

"I always liked him." Maybe because he was one
of the few upperclassmen who had given her the time
of day. Although he probably wouldn't have except
that he'd been a good friend of Savannah's. Along with
being the boyfriend of Savannah's closest friend—now
his wife—Della. Della, who also happened to be Linc's
sister-in-law. Small towns were like braided rugs—they
tended to weave everybody in together one way or another.

"Bucky's our only announcer. Has been for, oh, I'd
say a dozen or more years now. I guess he's the voice
of Elk Creek," Cully offered with a chuckle because
it sounded too grandiose for an informal speck on the
map with barely eighteen hundred citizens.

It was information about Della's husband that Ivey
knew because she and Savannah still saw a lot of
Della—albeit only in Cheyenne. But Cully had no way
of realizing that.

It was nice to hear Bucky's voice, though, Ivey
thought. Nice to feel so wanted, so at home in this
place she'd been in a hurry to leave.

Cully drove into Elk Creek proper then. Cheyenne
was northeast of Elk Creek so coming back to her cous-

ins' ranch after the wedding hadn't taken her through it. But now Ivey took it all in for the first time in fifteen years.

It was a homespun little town, she thought as they entered the north end of it. They passed the three-story school first and turned onto the circular drive that wrapped around the park square—the gazeboed sight of many of the warm-weather holiday celebrations. Across from it was an imposing courthouse with a tall clock tower, an old redbrick Georgian mansion that had been turned into a medical facility, and a steepled church, all of them watching over the park like sober sentries.

Tall Victorian street lamps lit the way as the circle merged into Center Street and ran southward to divide the town right down the middle and form the business district. Stately old stone, brick and weathered wood buildings lined either side of the main thoroughfare that was wide enough for two lanes of traffic and cars to park nose first in front of the offices and shops.

Ivey had forgotten what an eclectic group of buildings housed those offices and shops. Everything from country cottages to flat-faced boxes two and three stories high, to some clapboard structures that looked as if they'd been moved straight off the set of a Western movie.

A lot of the businesses in Elk Creek had changed, Ivey noticed. Some only in small ways, like proprietorship having passed down from parent to child, while others had disappeared altogether, and still other completely new establishments had sprouted among the old.

There hadn't been a movie theater before. Or the small dress boutique or specialty shop that sold maternity and baby things. There hadn't been the ice-cream parlor or an attorney in residence.

But enough of it remained the same so that she knew she could still find her way around. The bakery, the butcher shops, the jewelry and hardware stores, the insurance and real estate offices hadn't done more than add decorative shutters to the windows, a fresh coat of paint to the siding, or update a sign here and there. The veterinarian hadn't changed names or locations. Neither had the Western-wear shop, the appliance center, or the Laundromat and dry cleaners. And of course the Daye family's general store was right where it had always been, only now Kansas owned it instead of her mother and father.

But more important than the details of what had changed and what had remained the same, Ivey could feel that the essence of Elk Creek was still there. The friendliness she saw in folks waving to one another or standing on the sidewalks talking and laughing, clapping other folks on the back.

And it occurred to her that while she hadn't grown up in a warm, cozy home, there'd been solace outside of the house. In neighbors and friends and the people of the small town. Solace it felt good to be back in the center of again.

Margie Wilson's café was on the ground floor of one of those old clapboard buildings about three-quarters down Center Street. It was painted a pale yellow, trimmed in white, and sported a neon sign above the plate glass window in front.

Everybody knew Ivey's uncle Shag had had a back-door relationship with the café owner. Shag had been slightly less irascible than Silas, and Ivey had always wondered if indulging in the company of a woman might have softened her father some. But he'd never let himself get involved. To her knowledge anyway. If he had secretly, it hadn't helped.

"Are Hellers still allowed in here since Shag threw Margie Wilson over for that woman in Denver?" Ivey asked Cully when he'd parked the truck in front of the café.

"I've never heard of Margie turnin' anybody away. But nobody mentions your old uncle to her, so I wouldn't do that."

Ivey stared at the place for a moment, letting good memories drift through her mind. "I worked here the last summer I was in town, you know."

"No, I didn't know that. But my restaurant of choice then was the Dairy King. Did you wait tables?"

"I washed dishes. And swept up after closing. It gave me my stake for moving away the next June after graduation."

"You say that like you're still grateful for it all these years later. You must have really wanted out."

"Mmm," was all she said to confirm it.

Cully turned off the engine and as he came around the truck Ivey climbed down from the cab on her own to avoid the dilemma of his help.

Maybe he realized what she was doing and why, because once he was beside her he seemed to reach for her elbow as if to take it but thought better of it before he did. Instead he just held out his hand in a gesture that told her to go into the restaurant ahead of him.

Margie Wilson always did a good business but it was nearly seven-thirty by then and in Elk Creek that was late for the evening meal so there was a fair share of empty tables.

Nearly everyone in the place greeted Cully but not

a soul recognized Ivey. It didn't surprise her. Sometimes she saw pictures from those days she'd spent here and found it hard to recognize herself, too.

Funny, chopped-off hair; ragtag blue jeans; men's shirts that hid any evidence that she was female; and no makeup to even begin to hide her freckles or accentuate her features. It was actually a compliment that one glance at her didn't spur anyone's memory.

Margie Wilson wasn't there. Cully exchanged some small talk with the woman who seated them and introduced her to Ivey, but the waitress was far more interested in flirting with Cully than in meeting Ivey.

It rubbed Ivey wrong.

Not that Cully was anything more than congenial, but it still irritated Ivey and she was more intent on that than on trying to put a name to any of the faces she passed on the way to their table.

"Should I know her?" Ivey asked when the other woman had handed them menus and gone to pour more coffee for another table.

"She just moved to town a few years ago." He leaned forward and Ivey was treated to that clean-smelling aftershave again as he went on as if confiding in her, "Bad reputation. She's had affairs with two married men since she got here."

"Looks like she has her cap set for a single one now," Ivey muttered under her breath.

"I hope you don't mean me because I'm not interested in her," he said the same way, mimicking Ivey's muttering to tease her and clearly enjoying himself as he did.

The same woman was their waitress and came back before they'd barely had time to look at the menu. But they gave her their order anyway, prompting her to follow it up with such attentive service that until their food arrived, Cully and Ivey didn't have enough of a gap without her attendance to say five words to each other.

Finally, once Ivey's roast beef and Cully's steak were in front of them, Cully politely told the woman that they wouldn't be needing anything for a while and got them a breather from the overeager waitress.

That was when Ivey began to actually look around at the other diners. "Do I know any of these people?" she asked Cully quietly.

He looked around, too, but with a more subjective gaze now, judging who was who among the crowd that had thinned considerably just since they'd arrived.

While they ate he brought her up-to-date on those folks he thought she probably knew or knew in connection with someone else. It was an entertaining way to spend the meal because Cully made it informative and interesting without indulging in gossip.

As they were winding down with pie and coffee for dessert two more customers came into the café and took a booth near the door. Two customers whom Ivey initially thought were both men.

"Melanie Jorgenson," Cully said, putting a name—and gender—to one of them.

Ivey remembered Melanie Jorgenson, all right. She'd been Ivey's greatest fear of what she might grow into if she stayed in her father's house—more than a tomboy, a woman whose appearance was so masculine it didn't seem as if even Melanie knew she was a girl.

"That's her husband with her," Cully added. "You wouldn't know him. She met him at the stock show in Denver a few years back."

"I suffered a lot of ribbing about Melanie Jorgen-

son,'' Ivey said, glancing away from the other woman.
Ivey was glad Melanie had found a man who could see
beyond the surface.

''Why was that?''

''Because everybody thought Savannah and I were
just like her.''

He looked from Ivey to Melanie Jorgenson and back
again. ''I don't see the similarity.''

''Maybe not now. But—''

The waitress had started to reappear every few
minutes again and before Ivey could finish her sen-
tence, there she was once more. Only this time Cully
asked for the check and paid it before Ivey could de-
bate with him about who was going to treat for the
dinner.

Then he stood and said, ''If we don't get out of here
I'm going to be rude to this bird dog of a woman.''

He asked a busboy on the way out of the café to
load Ivey's groceries into the back of his truck and then
suggested they take a walk while it was being done.
''We can go down toward the train station and let you
have a look at Linc's honky-tonk.''

Ivey was only too happy to leave the waitress's do-
main and step out into the evening air. They headed
down Center Street on foot.

Proving he'd been listening to what she was saying
before, Cully said, ''So tell me how you and Melanie
Jorgenson were alike.''

''Come on, how do you think we were alike? Everybody used to mistake me for a boy, too.''

He grinned sheepishly.

''See—you did, didn't you?''

''Well, maybe once or twice. Seemed like that's how

you wanted it, with the way you dressed and wore your hair.''

"Ha! Hardly. That was how my father wanted it."

Cully's grin turned one-sided. "Well, as the father of two girls, I can see where it might feel safer to disguise 'em. Could be a good way to keep the boys from comin' around."

"That wasn't my father's reason."

"What was?"

"Silas never got over Savannah and my being girls. He seemed to think if he treated us like boys, made us dress like boys, worked us harder than boys, he could turn us into boys."

"I'm sure glad he didn't make it," Cully said, giving her an appreciative sidelong glance.

They'd reached the end of Center Street by then and looked to the east onto the train station that was closed for the night and the former holding barn across from it that now proclaimed itself The Bucking Bronco in bright letters above the open great door that spilled light and music from inside.

"Want to go down and say hello to Linc?" Cully asked.

Ivey did want to see her cousin's place of business but at that moment it was so nice to be out in the cool, quiet night, talking to Cully in a way that finally put her completely at ease.

"Another time maybe. I was kind of liking things just the way they've been."

He grinned again as if he were glad to hear that.

Then they crossed the road and walked back up Center Street from there.

"So," Cully began again, and even in just that single word she knew he was about to tease her once more.

"Are you tellin' me that ornery old Silas Heller was to blame for that hairdo you used to wear?"

Ivey moaned and laughed at the same time. "Wasn't that horrible? He said he wasn't paying good money for *girlie hair*—that's what he called it anytime we wanted to go into town to have a real haircut. Or even when we asked for shampoo—he used to make us wash our hair with the soap in the shower. I can't tell you how awful deodorant soap is on curly, unmanageable hair. And he wouldn't let us grow it out, either. Said he wasn't having us molting and clogging up his drains, or shedding hair into his food. Once a month or so he'd stick a bowl on our heads, snip off anything that hung below it, then do a quick cleanup with the sheep shears. Lord, it was like torture when we were teenagers."

"I'm surprised you stood for it."

"You don't know what it was like living with that man. Savannah and I banded together once and refused, and he hog-tied us and shaved our whole heads."

"No," Cully breathed in disbelief. "I would have remembered two bald girls hanging around town."

"It was in the summertime, right after school let out. We'd thought to let our hair grow through the vacation and surprise everybody with *girlie hair* when we started again in the fall. As it was, we ended up hiding out the whole time and going back with barely an inch and a half grown back. After that we just gritted our teeth when he got out the hair-cutting bowl and the sheep shears and gave in."

Cully laughed sympathetically, a rich sound that seeped into her pores and heated her insides like warm brandy.

"No wonder you were so funny lookin'," he said without apology.

"Thanks for noticing," she answered, laughing herself now that time made it all just an impotent old memory.

They only talked about the shops and businesses they passed for a while and then there they were, back at his truck, her groceries in boxes in the rear of it.

"We'd better get this stuff home before it spoils," he said in a way that made the two of them sound like a couple.

It sent a little thrill through Ivey that she didn't understand.

For the second time he opened the truck's passenger door for her and offered her a hand up. Only by then she was feeling so comfortable with him that she accepted it without thinking. And what she found was that she hadn't been imagining the electrically charged response his touch set off in her because it came again, even stronger than it had been before.

Strong enough that she hated losing it when he let her hand go to close the door between them.

Then he went around the front of the truck to the driver's side and she followed him with her eyes, enjoying the sight. That was when it occurred to her that this dinner had been a date, all right. A very pleasant date. One she was not happy to see coming to a close.

Cully got in, started the engine and then stretched a long arm across the rear of the seat as he backed out of the parking place.

She knew it was silly, but she couldn't help wishing that he'd leave that arm there as they headed out of town, reach for her and pull her closer to him on the seat so that he could wrap it around her.

Of course that didn't happen, but for a moment she lost herself in the fantasy, imagining what it would feel like to have that muscular arm resting along her back, one of those big, powerful hands clasping her shoulder, his solid side against her own, the scent of his after-shave wafting all around her, the warmth of his breath in her hair....

"Do you miss anything about livin' around here?"

With a bit of a jolt she forced herself out of her reverie. It took a few seconds for his words to register but once they had she said, "I didn't think I missed anything, no. At least not until tonight."

"And tonight you do?"

"It's just that it's felt better to be back than I expected it to. Good, even. I guess whenever I thought about Elk Creek, I thought about my father and the two were so jumbled together that it seemed like I hated this place."

Cully took his eyes off the road to look at her thoughtfully. "Does that mean you hated your father?"

"That sounds so terrible," she demurred with a cha-grined little laugh. "No, I didn't *hate* him. But there wasn't a lot of love in our house, either. Shag was tough on Linc and Jackson and Beth. Tough enough that it might be called abusive by today's standards. But he wasn't bitter. Silas was bitter. Sometimes it felt like he hated me. Hated Savannah."

"Just for being born girls?"

"For being born girls. Maybe for being born at all. For his being left to raise us alone. For who knows what else. He was an unhappy man."

Cully turned the truck onto the road leading to her house and Ivey forced a light laugh to chase away the rest of the memories she didn't want to dwell on.

"Well, that was a cheery ending to things, wasn't it? But to go back and answer your question about missing Elk Creek, I never did, but I'm finding the peace and quiet pretty appealing all of a sudden."

Almost as appealing as she was finding Cully, but she didn't say that.

It occurred to her that he was a combination of her two cousins. He could be as steadfast, hardworking, intent and intense as Jackson; and as full of pure, incorrigible charm as Linc.

It was a potent mix that she knew she shouldn't be liking so much and she reminded herself to guard against it.

Cully pulled up in front of the porch and while Ivey unlocked the front door and turned on lights inside, he carried in her groceries.

"Would you like a nightcap?" she offered when he had everything sitting on the kitchen table. "Kansas doesn't sell liquor but I had her put in some chamomile tea..."

That sounded pretty lame, but it was the only thing she could think of to get him to stay even a little longer.

Unfortunately it didn't work.

"Thanks, but I should be gettin' home," he said. "I've been gone a long time today."

Gone from his kids, Ivey thought, having forgotten about them and feeling slightly guilty for it.

"So we're still on for baby-sitting and saddle breakin' tomorrow?" he asked as he retraced his steps to her front door.

"Absolutely," she assured, following him and trying to keep her eyes off his very, very fine derriere.

"I need to do some work around home in the morning. So how about if we come over just after lunch-time?"

"I'll be here." No doubt waiting much too anxiously...

"Good," he murmured, pushing the screen door open with one of those big hands splayed against the frame. But he just held it that way, without going through it, and angled back toward her.

His piercing blue eyes seemed to study her face as he said almost cautiously, "This was nice."

"It was," she agreed in a soft voice, because she couldn't help thinking about how dates usually ended.

Was he going to kiss her? she wondered, hating how much she hoped he was.

And she really thought he would as he went on looking at her, holding her eyes with his.

But then all of a sudden he straightened up a little, veering back as if he'd been drawn to her and managed to resist at the last moment.

"We'll see you tomorrow then," he said in a voice more ragged than it had been before.

"Okay. I'll be looking forward to it...I mean to meeting your girls."

He nodded, smiling only slightly, as if he knew exactly what she'd be looking forward to and it didn't have anything to do with his kids.

"'Night," he said.

"Good night. Oh, and thanks for dinner and all your help today," she added, belatedly remembering her manners.

But he only nodded his oh-so-handsome head again and went out to his truck.

A gust of a sigh escaped Ivey's lungs all on its own

as she watched him go, and for yet another time today she suffered a wave of disappointment.

But he was right not to have kissed her, she told herself.

Right not to have crossed that line.

There was just one thing she didn't understand.

If it was so right, why did it feel so wrong?

Chapter Four

Ivey was crazy about kids. It really was the reason she'd become a teacher. And when she was away from her job—as she had been since the end of the previous school year in June—she missed being around them. So she was looking forward to meeting and spending some time with Cully's two daughters the next day.

Of course it didn't hurt that they *were* Cully's daughters, either.

Or that Cully would be with them.

But she didn't want to think too much about that.

She did some finish-up work around the house in the morning, putting off her shower until eleven so she'd be fresh when her company arrived. Then she dressed in a pair of trouser-cut jeans and a prim plaid blouse with a lace Peter Pan collar, and French braided her wet hair so it would be even more curly for her cousins' barbecue that evening.

She was downstairs watching for Cully and his kids by noon but it wasn't until twelve-thirty that she spotted the big white truck he'd picked her up in the night before coming along the rutted drive to stop right in front of the porch.

Ivey didn't want to appear overly anxious so she held back, spying from the curtains over a small side window in an alcove off the living room where her father's rolltop desk occupied most of the space.

Cully got out from behind the wheel and rounded the truck. He was wearing a plain whitewashed-on T-shirt—identical to the one he'd stripped down to the day before—tucked into a disreputable pair of snug jeans. The jeans were clean but so old there were holes haphazardly sewn in both knees and others left frayed around the edges of the seams and pockets, and when he turned his back to the house to open the passenger side of the truck, Ivey saw that one of his rear pockets was missing altogether.

He leaned into the truck's interior and she feasted on the sight of that to-die-for derriere while he released the seat belts and lifted down his daughters one by one.

They were two adorable little ragamuffins with the scraggliest blond hair Ivey had seen since her own early childhood when Silas hadn't even bothered with the bowl on her or Savannah's head before whacking their curls off. Both were dressed in red boys' T-shirts—the kind that came several to a package—and boys' overalls, with miniature cowboy boots on their feet.

It surprised Ivey. She'd expected little girls like she had in class—dressed in pink sweat suits or knit jumpers or blue jeans with appliques on the pockets, their hair done up in barrettes or elastic ruffles.

But these two children reminded her more of herself and Savannah at those young ages.

It gave a sort of twist to her heart to see it, even though the younger girl did an exuberant skip to the door and the older one held her dad's hand on the way, and neither seemed unhappy or as standoffish with their father as she and Savannah had been.

Still, they were girls dressed like boys and that set off some alarms in Ivey.

So many that she forgot about hiding her eagerness to see Cully again and rushed to the door to open it before he'd even reached it, wondering if she'd misjudged him and if his attitude toward his daughters was more like her father's than she thought.

"Hi!" the smallest cherub greeted her through the screen.

"Hi," Ivey answered, pushing it open and holding it with her hip while the little girl finished her skip with a flourish to stand directly before her.

"I'm Randa 'Lisabeth Culhane," the tiny child offered proudly.

Ivey couldn't help a smile as she stared down into enormous blue eyes just like Cully's. "Hi, Randa. I'm Ivey."

"I know. My daddy tol' us. Ivey—like what grows on the side of our house in the summer."

Cully and his other daughter drew up alongside Randa by then and he gently palmed the top of her head as if it were a signal to stop her from saying any more.

It worked, allowing him to introduce the other little girl who was watching Ivey from his side. "And this is Amy."

Ivey bent over and looked into another pair of pale blue eyes. "You're four, aren't you, Amy?"

She nodded her head of shoulder-length hair, sending some oddly angled strands into her eyes. "I had my birthday when it was the firecracker day," she informed, not as shy as Ivey thought she might be because she was holding Cully's hand. Now Ivey realized it was more proprietary. *This one is Daddy's girl,* she thought.

"I'm thirty-five—in case you were wondering," Cully said then, laughter and teasing in his voice, clearly to remind her he was there, too.

"But his birfday is when it snows," Randa offered matter-of-factly.

"I'll remember that," Ivey said, standing straight again to smile up into Cully's handsome face.

Although he was obviously dressed for work, his clothes were clean enough to tell her he'd just put them on. His face looked freshly shaved and he smelled of that scent she liked so much. The only sign that he'd spent the morning working was in the slight hat ring around his sable-colored hair. But even that didn't detract from his appeal.

With some difficulty, Ivey curbed her thoughts about how attractive he was even in clothes that weren't fit to be worn and invited them all in.

"We finded a dog here once when we comed over with our dad to feed the horses what stay in the barn here," Randa informed along the way.

"We din't getta keep 'im, though," Amy chimed in. "He belon'kt to somebody else and Daddy hadda give 'im back."

"Was he your dog?" Randa asked Ivey.

"No, it couldn't have been my dog. I haven't lived here in a long time."

"Do you got a dog?" Amy again.

"*Have* a dog," Cully corrected.

"Yeah, do ya?" Randa seconded, missing her father's grammatical correction altogether.

Ivey laughed. "No, I don't have a dog."

"We do." Amy once more. "He's a big one and—"

"Okay, okay," Cully cut in. "Can you guys save the dog talk for a minute?"

"We wasn't talkin' like dogs. Dogs bark like this—" Randa proceeded to demonstrate and again received the big hand on her head to stop her as Cully rolled his eyes at Ivey.

"I need to get to work," he said. "Think you can handle this?"

"I think so," Ivey answered with a grin to show how delightful she thought his daughters were even if she was sorry to lose his company to a horse.

"Mind if I go out through the back?"

"Be my guest."

He hesitated long enough to cast another charm-filled smile her way, but then seemed to force himself to glance down at his kids. "You girls behave yourselves, hear?"

Two heads of erratically chopped hair nodded.

"Don't bust yer butt," Randa advised.

Cully grimaced and said by way of explanation to Ivey, "One of my brothers' parting words."

Ivey just nodded her understanding. "A good sentiment, though."

That made his smile turn into a grin but all he said was, "If you need me just holler." Then he went around her, down the hall, through the kitchen and out the mudroom door, leaving Ivey alone with his daughters.

"Well, I was about to go upstairs and paint my fingernails," she confessed to her charges. It was an indulgence she hadn't gone without since leaving her father's house and his edict banning such foolishness. Not that she ever used anything but clear polish, but still, it never failed to make her feel pretty and feminine, and that seemed like a victory over Silas.

"Can we have our nails painted, too?" Amy asked, her eyes as wide as if something wondrous had just come within her grasp.

"Hold out your hands and let me take a look."

They did, presenting four tiny mitts that seemed to have been washed very recently.

Was this something she needed to holler for Cully about?

She knew he was busy and hated the thought of bothering him with something so small. Besides, as a teacher she was accustomed to making impromptu decisions about kids.

"Okay, I think it'll be all right," she said, hoping Cully wouldn't hit the ceiling about it the way her father would have, but reasoning that since the polish was clear he might never even notice.

She herded the two little girls upstairs to her room where she already had her manicure things set on the table that separated her bed from the one Savannah had used when they'd lived there together. As kids the table had acted as a combination nightstand-desk. It was situated against the wall, just below a window that looked out on the barn.

Okay, so she had an ulterior motive.

One glance out that window and she'd be able to see

everything Cully did in the paddock where his horse grazed.

That didn't mean it wasn't the best place for nail polishing.

"We never had our nails painted before," Amy announced as Ivey lifted each child to kneel on the bed on either side of the desk and took the chair in front of it for herself.

"Does your dad not like for you to?" she asked, having second thoughts about the wisdom of doing something that might get them into trouble.

Randa gave an elaborate shrug. "I don't think he cares. But he din't like for Amy to cut our hair."

Ah, so it had been Amy who had done the chop job.

Ivey was glad to know it hadn't been Cully.

"Randa's bangs was in her eyes and Daddy said he was needin' to cut 'em but never gettin' time to, so I did it," Amy defended herself.

"What did your dad think of that?" Ivey asked, aware of the clench her stomach went into every time she waited for one of the answers that could put Cully on a level with her own father.

"He jus' laughed and laughed, and said we look like we got our heads stuck in the thresher. Now we're gonna hafta go into town and get it all cut off short so's it can grow back nice 'cuz Daddy don't know what to do with it like this ways," Randa said.

Ivey's stomach unclenched. Cully might be dressing his daughters like boys the way her father had dressed her and Savannah, but at least he didn't have Silas's temper.

"Look! There he is!" Amy said suddenly, pointing a finger down toward the barn outside.

There Cully was all right. Coming out of the barn's

side door into the paddock. He had a blanket slung over one broad shoulder and carried a saddle braced against his hip, held there by an arm with biceps bulging against the restraint of his shirtsleeve. He approached the horse on that slightly bowlegged swagger, his hair shining in the sun.

And Ivey's heart did another sort of flip-flop, though this one had nothing whatsoever to do with him as a father.

"He's been workin' Toby with the bit and reins so Toby'll get used to 'em," Amy informed with authority. "But today he's gonna sit 'im for the first time."

Both of Cully's daughters stood on their knees, bracing themselves on the desktop to crane forward and get a look at their dad. So it wasn't too obvious when Ivey took up the middle spot to do the same.

Cully seemed to be talking to the animal, soothing it, rubbing its shoulder with a flattened hand in a way that the horse responded to by sidestepping nearer.

Cully kept it up—intermittently—as he threw the saddle blanket over the animal's back, pausing to do more of that calming caress, letting Toby get accustomed to the blanket before he put the saddle on top of it.

"Daddy said Toby's already pretty used to the saddle, jus' not to anybody ridin' in it," Amy explained as they all three stared raptly at Cully once more soothing the horse.

Ivey couldn't help staring at that hand on the animal's hide. Big. Strong. Long, thick, capable fingers...

Her own skin began to prickle with a longing to feel that touch, that caress. Her pulse was quick in her chest. And the room seemed much, much hotter than it had moments ago.

Cully took the reins that dangled from the bit in the animal's mouth and slowly raised them over its head.

More soothing massage. He seemed to be whispering in Toby's ear. And Ivey felt herself straining to read his lips, wanting to know what he was saying, to hear it herself, whispered in a soft gust of his warm breath against her skin....

He raised a booted foot to the stirrup and swung up into the saddle with a careful grace so as not to spook the animal, settling that taut derriere in the seat. Rugged, masculine, muscular, he was a sight to behold.

In fact, the pure, potent impact of watching him work with that animal stirred things in Ivey that she knew shouldn't be awakening. That she didn't want to awaken.

But there they were. In a way that seeing Arlen behind his desk at the bank had never done.

It seemed to take the horse a moment to realize what had happened, to feel the weight of Cully's solid body on its back.

Then it rebelled with a sudden force, rearing up.

Cully was ready for it and wasn't unseated. Instead he braced himself and absorbed the second buck. Then the third.

The horse took off at a run for several feet as if it could shake off the rider that way, pausing here and there to try yet another buck.

Still it had no success dislodging Cully.

Again and again it reared, ran, reared, all to no avail, until it suddenly yanked its front legs into the air so far up it stood straight, throwing Cully to the ground with a thud hard enough for even Ivey, Amy and Randa to hear through the window glass.

"Did he bust 'is butt?" Randa asked without any real concern.

But Ivey's concern was definitely real. It came in the perspiration that dotted her upper lip, the pounding of her pulse in her ears, the urge to run out of that room, down the stairs, through the house to the paddock, to Cully....

But as if in answer to his daughter's question, he stood up, slapped dirt out of first the thighs of his jeans, then the backside, and started over again, approaching the horse slowly, talking to it as he did.

Toby eyed him suspiciously, but didn't run from him, and once Cully had a hold of the reins, he again began the soothing caress of the animal's neck and shoulder, the talking to it in what looked like a lover's whisper.

"Nope, didn't bust 'is butt," Randa decreed. Then she knelt back down on the bed and said, "I thought we were gonna get our nails painted."

Even Amy lost interest in what her father was doing outside and turned her attention to the manicure things on the desk.

For Ivey, tearing her eyes away from Cully wasn't so easy. Even once she realized he wasn't hurt, she just went back to wanting to watch him.

But she was supposed to be watching his daughters, she reminded herself.

Besides, she couldn't really be interested in the man. Not so soon after leaving Arlen at the altar. Not when she had so many doubts about her own ability to genuinely fall in the bells-and-whistles kind of love and make a commitment. Not when she couldn't trust her own judgment of men.

Yet in her mind she could hear her sister's voice

goading her much the way Randa and Amy were bantering back and forth on either side of her.

Interested in Cully? No, she wasn't interested in Cully.

Not much she wasn't.

October was Ivey's favorite month. Especially early October, before autumn had begun its rush into winter. The days warmed to the seventies. Night temperatures danced with the forties, but took their time getting there.

Keeping in mind that they would get there, though, and that she was headed for an outdoor party that evening, Ivey wore black wool slacks, a lightweight sweater-vest over a plain silver-gray T-shirt, and a black blazer on top of that to match the slacks.

Taken out of the French braid, her hair was a riot of curls that cascaded around her face and neck, bounced against her shoulders and down her back. She added some gold hoop earrings to her lobes even though they only peeked out of the curls periodically when she moved her head, but she thought they gave her a bit of panache.

Dressed and ready to go, she wouldn't have minded walking across the road to Jackson's house, but Linc had called and insisted he and Kansas pick her up on their way. She was watching for them and stepped out onto the porch when she saw her cousin's red truck coming up the drive.

His wife, Kansas, took Linc's three-year-old son, Danny, onto her lap and slid to the center of the bench seat to make room for Ivey to get in.

Greetings were exchanged all around, with the exception of Danny. He tucked his chin and gave Ivey a hard stare from beneath a frown, and no amount of cajoling from Linc or Kansas could get him to say hello.

In spite of not having been back to Elk Creek in so long a time, Ivey and Savannah had kept close contact with Linc, Jackson and Beth, seeing them whenever one of them was in the city.

Still, it felt good to be back with them on their own home turf, with everyone together at once, Ivey realized as they laughed about how much more Danny was like his sobersided uncle Jackson than he was like his carefree father.

Linc parked the truck around back near the garage of the big Heller house and they went into the kitchen from there.

Jackson, Ally and Ally's eight-year-old daughter, Meggie, along with Beth, her husband, Ash, and their new baby, were all waiting inside, and the warmth and sense of family that Ivey met from them made her sorry she'd stayed away so long.

Besides, her cousins were fun. Even Jackson had loosened up since his marriage and joined in the teasing that no one was exempt from.

Seeing the three happy couples who had all conquered obstacles to their being together also gave Ivey a sense of hope that some relationships really did work out, even if hers hadn't.

Kansas's sister, Della, her husband, Bucky Dennehy—the local disc jockey—and their four kids were the first of the guests to show up.

Ivey had seen and talked to Della almost as much as she had her cousins since leaving Elk Creek. Della and Savannah had maintained their friendship, which meant that Ivey had spoken to Della on the phone whenever she'd happened to answer one of Della's calls to Savannah, and spent many an hour with Della and Savannah when Della had come to stay with them in Cheyenne for visits.

Ivey hadn't seen much of Della's husband or children, though, so that was where she concentrated her attention until the house began to fill with other old friends and acquaintances who wanted to say hello.

The kitchen got fuller and fuller until finally Linc shooed everyone onto the patio—a huge brick-paved area where numerous tables, lawn chairs and loungers were ready for their last fling of the season.

An enormous barbecue pit had been fenced off to keep any kids from falling into it, and a big bonfire built inside, even though it wasn't going to be used for cooking. It acted as an outdoor furnace to keep the evening's chill at bay.

Beside it was a bricked-in barbecue with a five-foot-long grill that was already red-hot from the coals below it and ready for the steaks, ribs, hot dogs and hamburgers that were the main course.

Even the yard began to be wall-to-wall bodies as it seemed half of Elk Creek came. Ivey saw folks she hadn't thought about in years and years. But in the crowd of people, she was still keeping watch for a particular face that never seemed to appear.

She'd asked Amy and Randa that afternoon if they were coming to the party tonight, but they hadn't had any idea what she was talking about. And by the time Cully had been ready to leave for the day, he'd been so full of dirt, grime and sweat from being repeatedly thrown by his horse that he hadn't paused for chitchat, but only taken his girls from where Ivey was playing tag with them out front, thanked her and left.

So he might not be coming, she had to admit to herself, however reluctantly.

After all, the barbecue was for people to get together with her again after so many years away and Cully had already done that. Plus he'd looked wrung out by his afternoon's chore. Why shower, dress and leave home again just to see someone he'd already seen three days in a row?

And somehow, the more likely it seemed that he wasn't going to show up, the more Ivey's enjoyment of the party tapered off.

It was silly, she knew. She wasn't there to be with Cully. She shouldn't even have been thinking about him. She should have been lost in catching up with so many other friends.

But the truth was that in the back of her mind this evening's festivities had meant only one thing to her— that she'd have another reason to see him. Without him, she just couldn't seem to find any enthusiasm for it.

Then, just when she'd begun to think this might be a very long evening, she spotted Amy and Randa.

They were dressed in blue jeans and boys' Western shirts, their hair still a jumble of odd angles. But there they were, running toward the other kids who were playing on an elaborate jungle gym that Jackson had only recently erected halfway between the main house and the old bunkhouse that Beth and her husband had remodeled into their home.

Just seeing Amy and Randa made Ivey's hopes take flight and cost her even the partial attention she'd been paying to the mayor's wife's discussion of who would judge the pickle competition at the town's upcoming Harvest Festival.

As soon as Ivey could do it politely, she excused

herself and began to work her way toward the house, scanning every face for the only one she really wanted to see, all the while afraid Cully's daughters might have come with their uncles, that Cully still might not be there.

Then she spotted him. Barely out the kitchen's sliding glass door, standing with Linc, Jackson and two other men who could only be his brothers.

The Culhane brothers. Cully, Clint and Yance. One as jaw-droppingly gorgeous as the other.

There was a strong resemblance among the three. They were all big, rock-solid men so close to the same height that mere fractions of an inch were the only difference, and they all had that sable-colored hair with touches of red shot through it.

There were distinctions in their features that characterized each of them—a nose that was more aquiline, a face narrower, lips fuller—but none of it left a doubt they were brothers or did harm to how handsome they were. Not by a long shot.

And they all had those eyes. Those strikingly beautiful, penetrating, observant, pale, pale blue eyes...

But it didn't matter to Ivey.

The only Culhane brother she was looking for was Cully. And even standing there between his equally attractive brothers, it was Cully who made her heart skip a beat.

This had really gotten out of hand, she told herself. Her pleasure in this evening shouldn't have been hinging on Cully's being there. And now that he was, it shouldn't matter to her, let alone alter the pace of her pulse.

But it did. *He* did. And fight it though she might, she couldn't change it.

It would have been awkward for her to break into the all-male group the Culhanes and her cousins formed, so Ivey decided to bypass them, to go into the house instead.

As she did she caught Cully's eye—not intentionally, she just happened to glance at him and find him watching her from over Jackson's shoulder.

She said a quiet hi and received a simple raising of his chin in acknowledgment. But he didn't seem inclined to leave the conversation going on among the five friends to do more than that, so she went the rest of the way inside as if seeing him again didn't mean any more to her than seeing her again apparently meant to him.

And that was how the next two hours went, all through dinner, dessert and a lot more mingling, reminiscing and remembering.

Cully kept his distance.

Ivey kept hers.

But that didn't mean she wasn't acutely aware of him the whole time.

To look at him, nobody would guess what kind of an afternoon he'd had. He seemed as fresh as if he'd spent the day lounging on the couch watching television—all clean shaven, no hair out of place, eyes alert, not a sign of fatigue.

He wore a much better pair of blue jeans over snakeskin cowboy boots, and a tan shirt with a short banded collar beneath a brown leather vest.

Pure cowboy. All potent masculinity.

And there didn't seem to be a single woman in attendance who overlooked it.

At least that's how it seemed to Ivey, since whenever her gaze settled on him there was another female guest nearby, laughing over something he'd said, smiling coyly up at him, or touching him in some way—a hand on his arm as leverage to lean forward and bestow a confidence, a palm on his chest to brace a giddy giggle.

No wonder he'd come tonight, she thought. It wasn't to see her. It was for the ego boost all that admiration must have given him. Although, to Cully's credit, Ivey never saw him seek out any one of the available women. Instead they seemed to find him wherever he went, like ants at a picnic.

But for Ivey, it helped keep anything like jealousy at bay. Especially when she would find Cully looking at her over the other women's heads rather than paying rapt attention to them. Watching her. Studying her. Almost tracking her as if to make sure he knew where she was at any given moment.

But the fact still remained that he never came near her. Never did more than incline his head when their eyes met. All the while a whole lot of other women got to talk to him, to be with him, to *touch* him....

Nine o'clock came and went before Ivey happened to speak to the other Culhanes, either. That was when Clint crossed her path and paused to say hello.

Clint was the middle brother—Savannah and Della's age at thirty-six.

"How's Savannah doin'?" he asked once the amenities were over.

So, Ivey thought, *he hasn't forgotten her any more than she's forgotten him.*

But that wasn't what she said. "Savannah's great. We share an apartment in Cheyenne."

"Guess that means she's single?"

"She is."

"Headed for the altar anytime soon?"

"No, not unless she met someone at my wedding a few days ago and something drastic happened."

"At your *almost* wedding," came the correction from behind her in a teasing tone.

"My *almost* wedding," she amended, taking no offense to the reminder because she was so glad to hear the voice it had come from—the unmistakable, deep, rich voice of Cully. She recognized it without even glancing over her shoulder.

But she did wonder why, after spending the whole evening away from her, he had chosen just that moment to give her the time of day.

Then it occurred to her that he probably hadn't. That he'd probably joined them to be with his brother instead of her, and the rush of joy that had washed through her the moment she'd heard his voice, ebbed.

And it didn't get any better when his next words seemed to prove it was his brother he'd come for. "Yance and the girls are all set to go," he said to Clint.

Clint nodded. "You comin'?"

"No, I think I'll stay a little longer. Catch a ride with somebody else. Or maybe walk," he added with a glance at Ivey.

She hated the fact that joy rushed through her again in an instant and that her evening took a turn for the better. But it did.

Then Cully said to Clint, "Sure you don't mind puttin' the girls to bed?"

"Nah. No big deal," Clint assured with a grin threatening to split his lips as if the two brothers were sharing a joke. Then, to Ivey, he said, "Tell Savannah I said hello."

"I'll do that. Tomorrow, as a matter of fact, since it seems Jackson is flying Cully into Cheyenne in the helicopter and I'm going along," she answered, surprising Cully and liking it, even if the mention of the trip Jackson had suggested she make with them sobered both brothers a bit.

Clint bid them good-night then and left, and for a moment neither Cully or Ivey did more than watch him go.

When he was out of sight, Ivey broke the silence. "I wasn't sure you'd come tonight. After the punishment you took from that horse this afternoon."

"What? A couple of falls? That wasn't punishment," he answered with a wry smile.

"And now you're going to walk home on top of it?"

"Thought I'd better."

"Why is that?"

"In case you are. Can't have you out alone after dark. Who knows what might happen to you? There's a shortage of women around these parts, you know."

"I thought people were safer out near small towns," she countered with a hint of aloofness to her voice, just to let him think she wasn't as thrilled with the prospect of him walking her home as she really was.

He gave her a mock frown and leaned forward slightly. "The only women who are safe in small towns are the mean or homely ones."

She could feel his breath against her ear, just the way she'd imagined as she'd watched him soothe his horse earlier in the day. And it felt every bit as good as she'd thought it would.

"So what do you say?" he asked, straightening up again—much to her dismay. "I gave you plenty of time to talk to every other living soul here tonight. How about giving me just a walk across the road?"

Goose bumps broke out along the surface of her skin

and she was glad she had on long sleeves so he couldn't see just how effective his charm was.

But still she felt bold enough to give him a little challenge. Or pretend to, at any rate.

"How do I know you aren't somebody women around these parts should be wary of?"

"You don't," he nearly whispered, raising one thick eyebrow raffishly.

Ivey couldn't help laughing at him. "So I'll be taking a risk if I let you walk me home?" A bigger risk than he knew—she was risking her heart even though her brain was shrieking caution.

"Live a little dangerously," he urged, meeting her eyes with his in a way that drew her in, held her....

"Okay," she heard herself say as if she didn't have a will of her own. But then, when it came to this man, she wasn't sure she did.

Cully grinned down at her, obviously pleased. "Whenever you're ready."

To leave was what he meant. But it sounded as if he were willing to wait for so much more.

Ivey tore her eyes away from his to glance around. The party had been breaking up for the past half hour. Most everyone had kids who needed to be taken home the way Amy and Randa had been, and tomorrow was a workday, which, in the country, meant a crack-of-dawn starting time. So the guests had dwindled to a scattered few cattlemen talking shop. But that left a mess behind that Kansas, Beth and Ally were already beginning to tackle.

"I should stay and help clean up," Ivey said.

But just as she did, Ally passed by, heard her and said, "Don't even think about it. The guest of honor doesn't do the dishes. Go on."

And that settled that.

Ivey made the rounds to say good-night and thank her cousins and their spouses for the party, and then there she was—stepping out of the artificial light of the patio into milky moon glow. With Cully.

They headed away from her cousins' house, not saying anything for a little while, the only sound that of their even steps on the gravel of the drive until Cully broke this second silence.

"Nice party."

"Mmm," she agreed. "It was good to see everybody again."

"Was Clint askin' about your sister?"

"I think that's the only reason he came over to say hello."

"Could be," Cully allowed without expanding on it.

"It didn't seem like anybody there tonight could count as a Culhane wife or girlfriend, or did I miss something?" she asked, making it sound as if she were inquiring more about his brothers than about him, when what she really wanted to know was if any one of the women who had flocked to Cully tonight had had a special place in his life.

"No wives and no girlfriends all the way around," he said.

Ivey waited for him to expand on that, too, but he didn't.

Instead he said, "I was surprised to hear you mention your wedding even just in passing. Didn't I stir up trouble for that the other night?"

It was a gentle goad accompanied by a hint of a smile and a sideways glance, and Ivey found herself less standoffish about the subject than she had been before.

"Oh, that's just old news by now," she joked.

"Does that mean you'll tell me what happened?"

"Does it matter?"

"Just wonderin'."

"And dying of curiosity," she goaded a little herself.

He grinned at her. "Guess we get used to knowin' everybody's business out here. You have to admit that it's a curiosity to have you show up after fifteen years just when you were supposed to be off gettin' married instead."

"Mmm," she repeated by way of admission.

She knew he could find out what had happened from any one of her cousins if only he asked them. She appreciated that he hadn't. That he'd waited to hear it from her. And she thought that restraint and respect for her privacy deserved some reward.

Besides, when she explored her own feelings about it, she realized she didn't mind telling him.

So she did. Honestly. Outlining exactly what she'd done in leaving Arlen at the altar.

What she didn't say was why.

And of course Cully wanted to know that, too.

"Maybe I'm just commitment-shy," she joked again in answer, but with a strong vein of her own recent concerns that it might be true. "I know that what was going through my mind as I was panicking was *till death do we part.* Till *death* do we part. And I couldn't face that idea."

She glanced at Cully as they crossed the road to her drive and even in the moonlight it was easy to see he was disturbed by what she'd said.

But looking over at his handsome profile was enough to stir things in her that had never been stirred by Arlen and that reaffirmed the other part of why she'd run from marrying him.

"Then, too, I just didn't hear bells and whistles," she added with a nervous laugh, remembering Arlen's response the last time she'd actually said that out loud and feeling a little afraid Cully might think it was as ridiculous.

But he didn't smirk or sneer or act as if he couldn't believe she'd said anything so idiotic. In fact, he nodded that gorgeous head of his as if he understood. "You didn't love him."

"I thought I did. A practical kind of love—short on passion, long on comfort. It seemed like that was the kind to get married with because maybe the passionate kind would fizzle out and I'd be left with nothing."

"Except you couldn't go through with it."

"Standing in that church, thinking about *till death do we part,* it already felt like nothing. So I couldn't go through with marrying him. It just wouldn't have been right. For either of us."

There didn't seem to be anything more to say about it. They walked along the rutted path to her house in silence for a while.

Ivey wondered if she was imagining it or if something about what she'd told Cully troubled him still. Not that she had any more than a sense of it because she couldn't read his features except to tell that he was thinking pretty seriously about something. And he was awfully quiet.

They'd reached her house and were climbing the porch stairs before he spoke again. "So you're going into Cheyenne with Jackson and me tomorrow, are you?"

Ivey had left the porch light on and they stepped

into its golden glimmer. It allowed her to see what the moon glow hadn't—that Cully had two vertical lines between his brows, telling her she'd been right about something not sitting well with him.

She just couldn't be sure at that point what it was. Or even if it had anything to do with what she'd told him about not going through with the wedding. Maybe he didn't want her along on his and Jackson's trip the next day.

"Jackson suggested it," she said. "He said there was room for me in the helicopter, and then once I get there I can pick up more of my things and drive my car back." What he hadn't said was why he and Cully were going into the city in the first place.

Cully nodded. "So you'll be driving back."

"That's the plan."

"But you *are* coming back."

Was that what was on his mind? That she might stay in Cheyenne once she got there? Did he care if she did? It was a nice possibility to entertain.

"What do you think? That I broke your back yesterday to clean this place and then won't stick around to use it?" she joked once more as she unlocked the front door.

When she turned to face him again he was smiling wryly down at her as if she'd guessed his secret.

"You Heller sisters are known for leavin' and not comin' home again."

"Yeah, but I've been kind of enjoying being home again." She hadn't intended to give herself away but somehow the message hung there in the air between them that her enjoyment had a whole lot to do with him.

And she wasn't just imagining it because Cully's

agile mouth again stretched into a grin—this one satisfied and knowing.

"Yeah, well, it's pretty good to have you back home," he said quietly, his eyes searching hers, holding them.

He raised one big hand to the side of her face then, cupping her jaw, running his thumb along the high crest of her cheekbone. His palm was calloused but not rough, the texture of kid leather, and as warm as she thought his vest probably was after a night of absorbing his body heat....

Better than a handshake, but not as good as a kiss, was what ran through Ivey's mind as she gazed up into those angular features and lost herself in the sensation of his touch. No wonder the horse had sidled in for more....

But just when she thought that was all he was going to do, his head started a slow descent her way.

He *was* going to kiss her.

Anticipation rose up in Ivey, drowning out the tiny voice in the back of her mind that said she shouldn't do this, shouldn't let him do this.

He paused a split second before reaching her, hovering a scant inch away, as if giving her that last moment to retreat.

But Ivey held her ground. She couldn't possibly have done anything else. Not when everything inside her was rooting for the kiss.

Then he closed the distance, his supple lips covering hers, but only softly, chastely, sweetly. More sweetly than she would have guessed a notorious rascal was capable of.

But all too soon he ended it, easing away from her even as his hand still caressed her face so tenderly.

"I guess I'll see you tomorrow," he said in a deep, husky, hushed voice.

"I guess," she countered, finding herself more light-headed from his kiss than she'd realized. And a lot more weak-kneed than such a single good-night buss should have left her.

Cully took his hand away in a slow, sensuous slide and then reached around her and opened the screen door she'd let shut after unlocking the mahogany one.

"Sleep tight," he said, waiting for her to go in.

"You, too," she heard herself answer as if in a daze.

She stepped inside when, in truth, she'd have rather had another kiss. Or maybe a hundred.

But once she was standing on the other side of the screen, Cully closed it. Firmly. And, as if to keep himself from doing more, he jammed his hands into the pockets of his jeans, leaving only two insolent thumbs sticking out and unconsciously pointing to that spot on his body she should not have been looking at....

Ivey yanked her eyes upward to his face and found yet another grin there, this one full of orneriness. "Lock your doors. Remember the dangers out here."

She could only nod. The dangers were all standing on her porch, in a tall, rock-hard package of masculinely glorious Culhane.

But she didn't say that. She just said, "'Night."

"'Night," he responded, his grin turning into a crooked smile.

And then he left, half bouncing down the steps on an energetic swagger that belied the full day's work he'd put in.

Ivey watched him head across her yard in the direction of his own property for as long as she could see him. Longer, as the image of him lingered in her mind.

And when she finally closed her door and went up to bed it was with only one thing in her thoughts.

That even that simple good-night kiss from Cully had roused more inside of her than the most passionate of Arlen's....

Chapter Five

As always, the next day Amy and Randa had Cully up early. The trouble was, by the time he'd fed and dressed them and they'd gone off with his brothers to play while Clint and Yance worked on a fence that was down, he'd also showered, shaved and dressed himself. So he ended up left home alone with nothing to do but put on his tie and wait for ten o'clock when he was set to be at Jackson's place.

Hard to escape thoughts he didn't want to have without anything else to occupy his mind.

This day had been a long time coming for him. And although it was overdue and he wasn't approaching it with the kind of raw emotions he would have had before this, it was still not something he was looking forward to. It was still a sad chore he was headed to Cheyenne to face.

He and Jackson and Ivey.

Not that Jackson and Ivey were going into the city for the same reason he was.

Jackson was doing him a favor and going as moral support because he was a good friend. Because he'd been through something pretty much the same.

And Ivey...Ivey was going to tend to her own business. She didn't even know what was happening with him.

But still and all, just remembering that she'd be along almost gave Cully a better feeling about making the trip. Although it probably shouldn't have.

"She left that man at the altar," he reminded his reflection in the mirror as he knotted his tie. And she'd said herself she was commitment-shy.

No, he definitely shouldn't be getting warm, happy feelings over a woman with *that* problem. Hadn't he learned anything from Kim?

Kim. The queen of commitment-shy women. It was the commitment to him, to the girls, that she couldn't follow through on. Too bad she hadn't left him at the altar. Everybody would have been a lot better off if she had.

So what the hell was he doing even giving a second thought to another woman who admitted to commitment problems? He should be putting a million miles between himself and Ivey. Himself, Amy, Randa and Ivey. He should be looking at Ivey with a jaundiced eye. He should be turned off by the very thought of her, the very sight of her.

But he wasn't.

No, here he was, thinking about her at every turn, every waking hour. Planning ways to see her again the minute he left her. Feeling like no amount of time with her was enough. Picturing her in his mind over and over—that wild curly hair, those violet eyes, those pale lips...

And even after hearing her say in her own words that she was commitment-shy, hadn't he gone and done what he'd been dying to do nearly since the first moment he'd set eyes on her? Hadn't he gone and *kissed* her?

Worse than that, hadn't he liked it so damn much he'd wanted to go on kissing her? Do a lot more than kiss her?

What could he have been thinking?

Just when he'd gotten himself and his girls back on an even keel again after being burned by Kim's commitment problems, how could he be attracted to another woman who admitted to commitment problems of her own? That was the last thing he needed to let into his life, into his daughters' lives.

"You should know better than anybody how it works," he said to his reflection again. "You get involved. You get in head over heels. And then out of the blue she's history and you're left hurtin'. Probably just like that fiancé of hers is hurtin' right now."

He couldn't let that happen again. No way.

"So you've had fair warning. Steer clear of her. Don't go walkin' her home at night. Hangin' 'round her porch, kissin' her..."

Damn, but it had been a good kiss, though.

If only she wasn't so all-fired pretty. And sweet. And nice. And funny. And easy to talk to, to be around. If only he didn't forget every single thing he should be remembering just as soon as he caught sight of her. If only he could stop thinking about more of that kissing—when he was with her and even when he wasn't. If only he could stop thinking about touching that soft, creamy skin of hers. About holding that small, perfect body against his. If only he didn't ache for wanting her as much as he did....

He finished tying his tie, leaving the knot hanging a few inches short of his collar, and braced both hands on either side of the sink to lean forward and stare hard at his own face in the mirror.

"Stay away from her," he ordered in no uncertain terms.

But in slightly less than an hour he'd be with her again. In Jackson's helicopter. On the way to Cheyenne.

He'd be able to smell her perfume again. He'd be able to hear her light, lilting voice again. He'd be able to see her smile, see the flash of spirit in those unusual eyes again. He'd be able to touch her by only reaching out....

"Stay away from her," he repeated, enunciating each word slowly, distinctly, as if he could make it sink in better that way.

But fast on that came another voice in his head.

Who did he think he was kidding?

He couldn't stay away from her.

Not just because circumstances might put them in the same proximity. But because he just plain didn't think he could make himself abide by that order.

He wanted to see her too much. To be with her.

"That's not the same thing as marrying her or needing some kind of commitment from her," he said in that more reasonable voice.

Could he spend some time with her and not get attached? Not expect anything permanent to come of it? Not get in too deep himself?

Hell, why not? Nobody said he had to marry her just because he spent some time with her. Kissed her.

He'd just be on guard. He'd just make damn sure he *didn't* get in too deep himself.

And in the meantime, he could enjoy her company, couldn't he? No harm in that. He'd earned it. So long as he watched himself.

Which might not be too easy when he was so busy watching her...

"It's the price you pay if you want to risk bein' with her," he warned his reflection. "Take it or leave it."

He considered that self-imposed ultimatum.

Did he want to be with someone he had to be careful of? Someone who put him at risk?

He must, because he wanted to be with Ivey.

"So I guess that means you're willin' to pay the price of bein' on guard with her to do it."

That's what it meant all right.

It had to.

Because the only alternative was not to be with her at all.

And when it came down to it, he knew he was only fooling himself to think he could resist the pull he felt toward her.

Ivey spent the whole trip into Cheyenne wondering one thing—why was Cully dressed in a suit and tie?

Not that he didn't look good in it.

The suit was a gray pinstripe, the tie was a plain pewter color, and he wore a crisp white shirt with it all, looking like any business executive might except for the black cowboy boots that poked out from beneath his well-tailored cuffs.

But neither Cully nor Jackson—who wasn't wearing

a suit but who did have on dress slacks and a dress shirt—offered an explanation for it. Not even when Ivey fished with compliments and comments and even asked if the two of them were headed for a funeral.

No, they weren't going to a funeral, Jackson had said, but that was the beginning and the end of the answer.

They had a rental car waiting at the airport but even without the drone of the helicopter's engine making conversation difficult, neither man offered more information and by the time they dropped her off in front of the apartment building where she and Savannah lived, her curiosity was still intact to take along with her inside.

"Hi, honey, I'm home," she called jokingly as she went into the third-floor apartment after using her key to open the first floor's security door, climbing the steps and unlocking the apartment door.

Savannah was in the hall-like kitchen to the right of the entrance and called back, "Hi, honey, I'm home, too."

Savannah hadn't lost quite as much as Ivey had of the tomboyishness they'd both grown up with. It still lurked around the edges in hair that had a bit of a windblown look to its long, very, very strawberry blond strands, and she rarely wore makeup even to hide her smattering of freckles.

But on Savannah it didn't matter. She was one of those natural beauties who could toss her head and her hair would look as good as if she'd worked at it. And her eyelashes were so long and thick they could well have been mascaraed.

Ivey envied that. Just as she envied her sister's take me or leave me as I am attitude. Savannah was not the people pleaser Ivey was. Savannah would not have put up with Arlen these last few months and gotten all the way to the altar before she told him to blow all his criticisms out his ear.

"Where's Jackson?" Savannah asked as she stepped around the breakfast bar, searching behind Ivey for signs of their cousin.

"He had somewhere to go with Cully, I guess. They just let me off, they didn't give me their itinerary." And the fact that it peeved her was in her tone.

"Oh, that's right. You told me Jackson was flying Cully into town—you were just the tagalong."

Which was exactly how she felt. And she didn't like it. Especially since Cully had been so preoccupied with whatever was on his mind that he had seemed only barely aware she was even with them.

"Are you going to spend the night or pack up and go right back?" Savannah asked then.

"Pack up and go right back. Want to come?"

Savannah was on sabbatical from the junior high school where she taught. She was working on her master's thesis, so her time was her own to schedule, as was the site she chose in which to work.

"You want me to go back to Elk Creek with you?" she asked as if she might not have heard Ivey right.

"You ought to. It would be a good place to write your paper—nice and quiet, peaceful, relaxed..."

"Sounds like you're really getting into it again."

"Actually, I think I am. Without Dad around to grump and growl and run things like the most miserable boot camp there is, it feels good to be there."

Savannah gave her a knowing glance. "Mm-hmmm. And how good is it all feeling because of Cully Culhane?'' she asked slyly. "I've noticed that his name keeps coming up every time I talk to you.''

"He doesn't have anything to do with it,'' she said as if it were a ridiculous notion. But in truth she knew there was some merit to it. Sure, she was rediscovering the benefits of small-town living—the slower pace, the friendlier people—but without Cully that slower pace might seem boring. And she was definitely enjoying his friendliness....

"Rebound, rebound, rebound,'' her sister chanted, seeing through her.

"I'm not on the rebound. Rebound is when someone dumps you. Not when you make the choice to end the relationship.''

"Just be careful, Ivey,'' Savannah beseeched. "I know how potent the Culhane brothers' attraction can be.''

"Speaking of Clint—''

"Which we weren't doing.''

"I saw him last night. He asked how you were. If you were married...'' Ivey let her voice trail off tantalizingly.

"Is he?'' Savannah asked as if someone were forcing her to against her will.

"Nope. No wives or girlfriends for any of the Culhanes.''

"Not possible. No Culhane goes womanless longer than fifteen minutes without some female clamoring to fill the vacant spot.''

"There are still a lot of women clamoring to fill the spots, but apparently the Culhanes aren't letting the spots be filled quite as easily as they used to. I watched all three of them dodging single women at my welcome home party last night.''

"Probably just an off night."

"I don't know...." Again her voice trailed away.

"Heard any more from Arlen?" Savannah asked, clearly changing the subject before talk of the Culhanes got any further.

Since Ivey wasn't particularly fond of her sister's goads about Cully, she didn't balk at it. "No, I haven't heard from Arlen. Not since I called him. Have you?"

"He came by here to pick up the garter his mother loaned you for the wedding. Acting like it was the crown jewels and you were trying to keep them."

"Did you give him the garter?"

"Sure."

"Good."

"Any regrets?"

"Not one. About calling off the wedding, anyway. I regret letting it get that far."

They'd moved into Ivey's bedroom by then and on to another subject Ivey didn't want to discuss.

So, while Savannah sat on her bed and Ivey folded clothes into a box she'd pulled down from the top of the closet, it was Ivey's turn to talk about something else.

"The Culhanes still want to buy us out. We should probably discuss it at some point."

"Seems to me we can't consider selling if you're living there."

"It's just temporary," she said forcefully. Then she wondered if she was trying to convince her sister or herself because she found herself feeling a bit of regret at the thought of leaving. The old house. Elk Creek. Cully...

"Are you sure it's only temporary?" Savannah asked, once more seeing through her.

"Maybe we could sell everything but the house and the acre or so around it," Ivey suggested rather than admit to her sister that she was feeling a twinge of something she didn't quite understand at the thought of staying in Elk Creek only for a little while.

"Maybe we better not agree to selling anything right now."

"Come back with me," Ivey said again. "See what you think."

"I don't know, Ivey...." This time it was Savannah whose voice dwindled away.

"Think about it, at least. We could go through the things in the house together, the way we should have when Dad died. You can work on your thesis and keep me company."

"Better company than Cully Culhane is keeping you?"

Back to that again. Ivey knew it was a safer topic for her sister than the idea of returning to Elk Creek herself and being anywhere near Clint Culhane, so she didn't pursue it as relentlessly as she might have something else and instead just playfully threw a blouse at Savannah.

"Quit giving me a hard time and help me pack. And promise you'll come down to the old homestead and just look around before we really think about selling."

Savannah made a face that said she didn't want to think about any of it and threw the blouse back at Ivey.

"Della would be thrilled," Ivey said as enticement. "You'd get to see her kids and Bucky—you know she's always complaining that you won't come see her."

"I'll *think* about it." But *only* think about it, was

what Savannah was saying. She wasn't agreeing to anything.

Still, it gave Ivey hope that she might lure her sister back to Elk Creek, even for a short visit.

And if she did, she'd have a distraction from Cully.

Which seemed like a good thing after the way he'd acted on their trip into Cheyenne today.

It was nearly four that afternoon before Ivey was completely packed, had her car almost loaded and was ready to go. But in the middle of her goodbyes and reminders to Savannah to think about coming to Elk Creek even just for a weekend, the buzzer on the apartment intercom sounded.

Ivey was closest to it so she pushed the speaker button to ask who it was.

Cully's voice came across the wire.

Ivey hid her surprise, said to come on up and pressed the door release. When she looked at her sister she found Savannah's eyebrows arched. "Well, well, well."

"He and Jackson are probably just wanting to know if I need anything to go back on the helicopter with them," Ivey said simply enough, hoping her sister couldn't tell that merely hearing Cully's voice and knowing he was on his way to her for whatever reason was enough to give her heart palpitations and make her every sense sit up and take notice.

"Mm-hmmm," Savannah murmured knowingly.

Ivey opened the door to Cully when they heard his footfalls on the last flight of stairs. Gone were the suit coat and tie; his collar was undone and his shirtsleeves were rolled to midforearm. And he looked much, much more relaxed than he had on the trip from Elk Creek.

In fact, he looked as if the weight of the world had been lifted from the big, broad shoulders that stretched his shirt.

He smiled at Ivey but caught sight of her sister before they'd said hello, pointing a long, thick finger at her.

"Savannah. I didn't know you'd be here," he said by way of greeting.

"I didn't know you'd be here, either," she countered.

"It's good to see you."

"You, too."

"Nice place," he continued with a quick dart of his eyes around what could be seen of the tiny apartment. "I understand you and Ivey live here together."

"Ever since we finished college. We've thought about moving—it's nothing plush and we could probably afford bigger and better now—but I guess we're kind of set in our ways." Savannah laughed slightly and then joked, "To tell the truth, I've worried some that that's why Ivey didn't go through with the wedding—because she couldn't leave me and this apartment. But I guess her staying in Elk Creek now knocks the stuffing out of that theory."

"Speaking of Elk Creek..." Cully glanced back at Ivey again but went on speaking to Savannah. "Thought I'd drive back with your sister here so she isn't making the trip alone."

It really wasn't fair that so little from him could set off so much inside Ivey, but there she stood feeling a thrill of delight dancing across the surface of her skin, trying hard to remember she'd been less than happy with him before.

"Is your business in Cheyenne all taken care of?"

she asked, hoping to sound somewhat aloof for both Cully's sake and Savannah's.

"All taken care of," he confirmed with a grin that said he looked upon the aloofness only as a challenge.

"And Jackson didn't mind flying back on his own?"

"Said he'd rest easier knowin' you weren't on the road by yourself."

"What if there isn't room in the car?"

He winked at her. "We'll make room."

Savannah nudged Ivey shoulder to shoulder. "Go on. I feel better knowing you won't be on the road alone, too."

Cully spotted one last box near the door, obviously meant for Ivey to take down with her. He pointed his prominent chin in that direction. "This going, too?"

"Mmm," she said with a nod.

"How 'bout I take it and wait for you outside?"

"Good idea," Savannah said before Ivey could.

Cully hoisted the box to one hip and then smiled at Savannah as if they were coconspirators. "You ought to come to old Elk Creek for a visit sometime soon. I know a few people would be *real* happy to see you again," he said by way of a goodbye.

And then he was gone and Ivey was left with her sister smiling like a Cheshire cat.

"My, my, *that* Culhane grew up well."

"They all did," Ivey countered.

"No doubt why *old* Elk Creek is looking better to you than it did before."

Ivey just rolled her eyes at her sister and did a little goading in return. "Come and see the rest of the sights for yourself."

"No room in the car," Savannah answered smugly. "But you two have a nice drive back."

"Think it over," Ivey urged, ignoring her sister's goad.

"Mmm," was all Savannah would concede as they finally said their goodbyes and Ivey followed Cully out.

Ivey's small blue compact sedan was parked nose first just outside the apartment house door, the trunk open for that last box. Cully was waiting for her there, sitting on the hood of the car, his long, work-hardened legs stretched out in front of him, one ankle lying casually atop the other, his arms crossed over his broad chest in a way that hid his hands but left the muscles of his bare forearms exposed.

"Hey, lady, want a ride?" he joked with a mockingly lascivious tone that was too intriguing to resist.

But Ivey tried anyway, remembering the nearly cold shoulder she'd gotten from him on the way to Cheyenne in the first place.

"I thought maybe you'd been taking me for a ride all week."

"Ouch! What'd I do to deserve that?"

Ivey didn't answer him. She just took that last box from where he'd set it on the hood beside him, put it in the trunk and closed the lid with a resounding slam. Then she went to the driver's-side door, unlocked it and got behind the wheel to start the engine.

It rumbled to life beneath Cully's very attractive derriere but he didn't move right away. He just stayed there, leaving his enticingly broad back blocking her view of anything else for a few minutes.

Then he pushed off the hood at a leisurely pace and came around to the driver's side, too.

He opened the door and held out his hand to her.

"What?" she asked.

"I haven't let a woman chauffeur me around since

the day I got my driver's license. I don't intend to start now," he said with a half grin that threatened to melt all the starch out of her joints.

Still, she tried to resist his appeal and said, "This happens to be my car and my trip to Elk Creek that you're insinuating yourself into."

"Even so."

He reached in, took one of her hands off the steering wheel and held it gently between both of his, rubbing the back with a tender, sensual stroke that set off tiny firecrackers in her stomach. Then he hunkered down to look her in the eye with those gorgeous ice blue ones of his that seemed to be glittering with delight, gave her a smile that she knew had gotten him anything he wanted from women most of his life, and in a quiet voice that was so sexy it seemed to sluice along her nerve endings, he said, "Don't make me have to yank your little rump outta there."

A laugh rolled from her throat all on its own.

"Come on, now," he coaxed in that dark honey-hued voice.

She considered putting up a fuss just on principle. But she had the sense that he'd love for her to do that so he could make good on his threat of horseplay. And wouldn't her neighbors love that!

Wanting to avoid a scene, she conceded. "All right. But this is silly."

"Silly or not," was all he answered, standing again and helping her out of the car with the hand that was still holding hers.

He walked her around to the passenger side like an old-world gentleman and opened that door for her.

"Buckle up," he ordered when she was in the seat, then he locked the door and closed it securely.

He went around the rear of the car, robbing Ivey of the sight of him. But she heard him give the lid of the trunk a victory tap as he passed it and she couldn't help smiling.

Cowboy macho, she thought.

But she liked it in spite of herself.

"Are we in any hurry to get back?" he asked as he got behind the wheel and adjusted the seat to accommodate his much greater size.

"I'm not," she answered.

"Good. Then we'll take the scenic route," he said as he put the car in reverse, reached an arm across the top of her seat and backed out of the parking space as smoothly as if he'd been driving her car the whole ten years she'd owned it.

The scenic route meant country roads instead of highway, past corn and wheat fields, past pastures and farmhouses, through tiny hole-in-the-wall towns that made Elk Creek seem like a metropolis, and past some red sandstone rock formations that looked as if a sculptor had carved them straight out of the earth.

But driving through it all in the crisp autumn evening was very relaxing, and with Cully doing the driving, Ivey rested her head and enjoyed the scenery. Outside the car and inside of it, too. Without saying much of anything.

Cully didn't seem to mind. In fact, with the exception of pointing out something worth seeing that she might otherwise miss, he was content with silence, too. But unlike the sober, introverted kind they'd flown to Cheyenne with, this silence was companionable and Ivey never had the sense that he'd forgotten for even a moment that she was there with him.

They were nearly back in Elk Creek before they

stopped at a roadside diner for dinner. The hamburgers were big and juicy, the french fries fresh cut, and the music coming from the jukebox too loud to do a lot of chatting there, either.

But once they were back in the car Cully seemed inclined to talk since he nodded at the loaded-up rear seat and finally said, "Looks like you're plannin' on stayin' a while."

"Oh, I don't know. It's really just all stuff I'll need even if it's only a couple of weeks—the weather could change to cold and snow anytime and I'd have to have warmer clothes. The TV is just a portable—for company. And this seems like a good chance to catch up on some reading I've been meaning to get around to."

But she had brought a lot, she admitted to herself only now. Enough to stay on a long while. If she decided to.

She didn't want to talk about that, though. And since being with her sister again had brought out a bit of Savannah-like boldness, she finally opted for a head-on approach to what had been driving her crazy all day long.

"So what exactly did you and Jackson do in Cheyenne?"

Cully kept his eyes straight ahead and didn't answer right away. Actually he let so much silence lapse that she began to wonder if he'd heard her.

Then, just when she was debating whether or not to repeat her question, he said, "I had to go to court. Jackson just kept me company."

"Are you in trouble?"

He chuckled at that. "Got my final divorce decree."

"Oh." That knocked some of the wind out of her. He hadn't talked about his wife or when she'd left.

Or why. But his *long gone* comment had had Ivey assuming the wife and the divorce were history. It was disconcerting to find they weren't. And it made her wonder how fresh his wounds were.

"You don't seem very broken up," she said somewhat tentatively, remembering that from the time she and Savannah had gotten old enough to ask anything about their mother, their father had acted as if it didn't matter to him one way or another. She'd always thought that she didn't ever want a man to care so little for her. Now she wondered if Cully could be as cold and uncaring as that.

He glanced at her from the corner of his eye. "I was plenty broken up about it. But she left before Randa was a month old. I've had a whole lot of time to get over it."

"What took so long to get to court?" Hey, if she was going to pry, she might as well go all the way. Besides, for some reason she didn't fully understand, she felt as if she had a stake in knowing the whole story.

"I've been tryin' to get it over and done with. But Kim isn't good with stickin' to things—in case you hadn't guessed."

"Didn't she want the divorce?"

"Oh, she wanted it all right. She made that real clear. She did the filing in the first place. It's the follow-through she can't do. She started college, couldn't finish. Started a half-dozen different careers, couldn't stay with any of them. Married me, had the girls, couldn't keep on with that, either. The divorce was no different. Her life's no different—the few times I've heard from her she's always on to something, someone new that she swears is finally just what she wants, just where she's meant to be goin', just what she knows without a doubt she should be doin'. Next time I talk to her, she's forgotten all about it and is all het up over a new scheme, a new man, a new job, a new life. She changes 'em like other people change their socks.''

He shook his head and chuckled mirthlessly but there didn't seem to be any anger left in him. It all spoke of simple, matter-of-fact acceptance—though not approval—of his ex-wife's weakness. Clearly it no longer had any power to hurt him.

"Who was she? Anyone from around Elk Creek?" Ivey asked then.

"No. Her name's Kim—Kim Billings. I met her at a cattle auction. Married her before I should have—I really barely knew her. But that didn't seem to matter at the time. I was head over heels in love with her and she was so enthusiastic, so damn sure I was what she wanted, too, that knowing her better didn't seem like a big deal." Again the chuckle and the head shake. "That's Kim. Always so damn enthusiastic and sure. At first. Until the blush wears off and the long haul is starin' her in the face. Then she's out the door."

"But she stayed long enough to have two kids," Ivey reminded.

"Barely. She was restless and hell-bent to leave the marriage within three months after the wedding. Just when we realized she was pregnant with Amy. I thought that might broaden her outlook some, finally get her to thinkin' about somebody other than herself for a change—even if it wasn't me."

"But it didn't?"

"No. Oh, she was full of that fickle enthusiasm while she was pregnant—decoratin' the nursery, shoppin' for baby things, swearin' she was goin' to be the best mother there ever was. But once the baby got here she resented the demands of a newborn. By the time Amy was a couple of months old Kim was wonderin' how she could get out of it all and make it not look bad to abandon her child. But then boom! She was pregnant again."

"And not happy about it."

"I had to fight like hell to keep her from having an abortion. That was what she wanted to do. She even went into town to arrange to have it done behind my back. I wouldn't have even known what she was up to if a friend she'd confided in hadn't come to me about it beforehand." Cully shook his head yet again, this time in what looked like disbelief at his own memory.

"I convinced her to go through with havin' the baby, but it was not a nice nine months," he continued a moment later. "By the time Randa was barely three weeks old Kim wasn't even worried anymore about how it would look—she was just out of there. Said bein' married and havin' kids wasn't as right for her as she'd thought it was."

"What about Amy and Randa?"

"She doesn't even want to see them. They're just part of that other phase she's moved on from—like the boyfriends and jobs and living arrangements she's left behind in the last few years. When she's lost interest it's over for her. She wants no reminders. She wants to start again, as if nothing else came before."

"Poor kids," Ivey muttered more to herself than to Cully.

"They got shortchanged in the mother department, that's for sure. And I'm to blame. I picked her."

Ivey thought about the afternoon she'd spent with Amy and Randa, about their adoration of their daddy.

"They seem to be doing okay," she said. Better than she and Savannah had done being brought up by a single father. Even if it did seem as though they were being raised as ersatz boys the same way.

"So that's how I spent today," Cully said into her wandering thoughts. "With Jackson walkin' me through the process of gettin' the divorce finalized because he's been there and he's a good friend. But now it's over and done with."

And that seemed to put an end to the conversation, too.

Especially when Ivey realized they were home again—his home—as he turned off the road onto the tree-lined drive that took them up to the Culhane house.

She'd been there only a few times as a kid and was impressed anew by the ranch house as they approached it. Like her own family home, it was clapboard, but that was about the only thing they shared in common.

The Culhanes' house was a sprawling two-story structure that stretched wide enough to fill nearly a whole city block. There were a full seven windows on either side of the front door on the lower level behind a front porch that looked more like the veranda of a Southern plantation house.

The upper level had a dormer that protruded from its center beneath a steep black-shingled roof that matched the shutters and trim in sharp contrast to the pristine white paint of the house. Out of that roof came six chimneys at various locations that made it clear no one would have to go far on a cold winter's day to find a fireplace to warm himself in front of.

And all around the house and on either side of the drive was a barbered lawn that would have done any big-city mansion proud.

"This place has held up well," Ivey said in understatement.

"Home sweet home," Cully agreed as he pulled to a stop in front of it where the drive formed a horseshoe back to the road again.

"What are you going to use my house for if we sell out? Kindling?" she joked.

"We've had some good years," he allowed. "Your little house isn't so bad, though. It needs an update but there's a lot of room for adding on to it. Clint and Yance and I have talked about it and we'd keep the house. Who knows, one of these days one of us might get a marriage to work and want to live away from the other two. Stranger things have happened, you know."

"Sounds like you guys have given a lot of thought to buying us out."

"We wouldn't have made the offer if we hadn't. But there's no rush."

"Good, because I'm not even sure after all these years what we'd be selling to you. For all I know there could be weeds far and wide, or secret oil wells that have sprouted up on the perimeters," she joked.

"Neither," he answered with a laugh. "Why don't you let me take you out tomorrow to look everything over? It'd give you some idea of what we're talkin' about."

It would also give her a chance to see him again, which would mean that not a day had gone by since she'd come back to Elk Creek that she hadn't spent some time with him.

Maybe that wasn't wise, a cautioning voice in the back of her mind said. Especially not when every hour she was with him made her like him all the more, made her all the more aware of every single thing about him and how attractive she found him, made her want all the more of his time and attention and a whole lot of other things...

On the other hand, she really should take a look at how the ranch had shaped up under the Culhanes' hands and what she and Savannah would be selling to them.

"That would be nice," she heard herself say, agreeing to his showing her around before that voice of caution could make a comeback.

"Trouble is I have some work that has to be taken care of for most of the day. What would you say to headin' out around four? Bringin' along a picnic supper? We should be able to cover everything before dark, then we'll build a campfire, eat and head back in?"

What would she say to that? She'd say it sounded more appealing than anything else she could have come up with on her own.

But she tried to keep that out of her voice. "Sounds fine," she said as if the very thought of it wasn't enough to keep her awake most of the night with the kind of anticipation a young girl would have for her first date.

An anticipation that was already at work making her ultraaware of Cully sitting so nearby in the small car, one hair-speckled forearm slung across the steering wheel as he angled toward her, his other arm stretched over the back of her seat, his massive thighs separated from her own by only the gearshift.

He hadn't had a hair out of place when she'd first seen him at Jackson's house this morning, or even when he'd shown up at her apartment this afternoon, but as he'd relaxed on the drive home there had been a time or two that he'd raked his hands through it so it was rakishly imperfect. Ivey liked it better than the earlier well-kept look. And his cheeks and the sharp line of his jaw were shadowed with the day's growth of beard, only adding to his masculine appeal.

She realized suddenly that they'd been sitting there in silence for several minutes, staring at each other. Cully seemed to be caressing her with his eyes, taking in every detail of her face, and approving of it if his secret smile was any indication.

He turned his hand from the seat back to her nape then, so softly his touch was a feather stroke under her hair.

"I suppose I should go in," he said in a quiet voice that made it clear he was reluctant to do it.

"Do you want me to walk you to your door?" she asked, joking again.

There was just enough light coming in from the tall pole lamps that lined the drive to let her see the glint that came into his eyes at that. "Not unless you were thinkin' of comin' in and whilin' away the whole night with me," he said, sounding as if he were daring her to.

"I think I'd better get home," she declined, ignoring the small thrill that rippled through her at just the thought of staying. "I'm sure your girls have missed you."

One thick eyebrow arched and his smile was full of the orneriness. "Even so," he repeated. Then, temptingly he added, "I tell a pretty fine bedtime story."

She couldn't resist a laugh at the pure devilry in his tone. "I'll have to pass."

"Chicken," he accused.

"Through and through," she agreed.

He took his hand away from her nape and got out of the car, coming around to open her door then, as if she really were going inside with him.

"Come on, I can't have you climbin' over that gearshift," he said, holding his hand out to her.

Of course, Ivey thought. But a dab of disappointment stabbed her anyway, as if a part of her had been hoping he might insist she go inside.

She took his hand without considering the wisdom in it, and felt a warmth slide from there up her arm and drip through her like hot lava.

He kept hold of it as he led her to the driver's side, but didn't let go once he got there, instead swinging her to face him.

"Can you still ride a horse?" he asked.

She knew he was referring to their plans for the next day, with more of that mischief in his expression as he gazed down into her eyes.

"It's been a long time, but I think so."

"Good. Then that's how we'll go out tomorrow."

Tomorrow...

It seemed so far away at that moment when all Ivey wanted was more of the present.

But just then the front door opened and Amy called out, "'S that you, Daddy?"

Cully didn't stop looking at Ivey even as he said, "It's me, all right."

"Are you comin' in?"

"Give me a minute, okay? Go pick a book for me to read tonight."

"Can't I come out there with you?"

He chuckled deep in his throat. "No, ma'am, you can not. Now close that door and wait for me upstairs."

Then to Ivey he said, "She's worse than a father tryin' to protect his daughter from a heartbreaker."

Ivey smiled up into his oh-so-handsome face, feeling that starch melting out of her joints again and leaning back against her car for support. "Are you a heartbreaker?"

His grin was crooked. "Not intentionally." He dipped down for a quick, playful peck of a kiss. "But if I am I'm in good company," he reminded, clearly meaning that she'd done her share of it in leaving Arlen at the altar.

It was hard to think of Arlen having a broken heart because it was hard to think of Arlen having much of a heart at all. But she didn't tell Cully that. Instead she said, "You should go in."

"Tryin' to get rid of me?"

Never.

But she didn't say that, either. "You promised."

"Mmm," he murmured, moving forward enough to brace both his arms on the car roof and lean in closer. "Promised myself somethin', too."

"What?"

He didn't answer with words. Rather he smiled yet again as he closed the distance between them to press his mouth to hers.

The kiss was soft, sweet, much like the one they'd shared the night before. But it didn't stay that way for long before he deepened it, before he parted his lips, before he urged hers to part, too.

The Culhanes had had reputations for a lot of things in school. Hell raising. Heart breaking. Being the best kissers around. Rumor had it that you hadn't really been kissed until you'd been kissed by a Culhane.

And suddenly Ivey knew why.

The man could work magic with his mouth. He could set off a whole Fourth of July inside her without so much as touching her in any way but that kiss that was just firm enough, just moist enough, just insistent enough, just masterful enough...

Her mind went blank; the whole earth could have fallen away under her feet, and she wouldn't have noticed, so lost in that kiss was she. In the sweet sexiness of it.

And then slowly he ended it, drawing away in stages that let her know he was going to, then following up with two more of those small, chaste pecks as if to seal it.

"Thanks for the ride home," he whispered in a tone that was cocky and at the same time husky enough to let her know she wasn't the only one whose socks had been knocked off by that kiss.

"Anytime," she heard herself whisper back in much the same way.

Then he did a sort of push-up to kiss her once more—playfully this time—before he took her by the shoulders to gently ease her away from the car, opened the door and urged her to get in behind the wheel.

Once she was there he reached in and barely brushed the crest of her cheekbone with a single knuckle before he said good-night, closed her door and headed for his house.

It took some effort but Ivey remembered to start the engine even as her eyes followed Cully, stuck like glue to that sexy swagger of his that turned her insides to mush.

How had any woman ever left that behind? she thought.

Then she laughed quietly at her own double entendre, feeling a little giddy.

And a lot light-headed.

And a lot more stirred up than she had any business being.

All over a man she should have been steering clear of, that cautioning voice reminded her.

Because nothing and no one who could wield that kind of power over her senses could be good for her.

But, cautioning voice or not, she knew she wasn't likely to steer clear of him.

Not when what she wanted more than anything was to be with him.

Chapter Six

Ivey spent the lion's share of the next day going through her father's room since Savannah had said to go ahead without her and had clearly not wanted to be in on the task.

Like her father, his room was cold and impersonal. Besides the double bed that Ivey finally made up and covered with the old chenille spread that had always been on it, the only other piece of furniture was a bureau filled with nondescript work clothes—overalls, shirts, underthings.

Nowhere in any of the drawers was there anything else, any souvenir from his boyhood, or medal from his time in the army fighting the Korean War, any sign of anything he might have taken pride in or pleasure in or that might have brought back a fond memory for him.

The top of the bureau was bare of any decorations

or reminders, too. It held only an old straight razor he'd used to shave his beard and the leather strop he'd sharpened it on.

He'd stopped keeping them in the bathroom after Savannah had tried to shave her legs with the razor—without a woman around to give lessons about such things Ivey and Savannah had been left to fend for themselves. Savannah's maiden attempt with Silas's straight razor had scraped her shin nearly to the bone and raised their father's ire. But then everything had raised their father's ire.

The town nurse who'd tended Savannah's wound had been the person who had finally given instructions about how to perform the personal chore. Instructions that Savannah had passed down to Ivey when the time had come. But even so, Silas had kept his razor in his room from then on.

No comb or brush kept the shaving things company because Silas hadn't owned either. There hadn't been a need since once every other week he'd buzz-cut his own hair so as not to have to bother with it.

There were no pictures on the walls. No mirrors. No mementos, no knickknacks. It was as if she and Savannah really had gone through the room after their father's death and cleared it of anything meaningful. But they hadn't. There just didn't seem to have ever been anything meaningful stored there.

Ivey made a trip into her own room for two of the boxes she'd carted some of her things in from Cheyenne. She emptied her father's drawers into them so the clothes could be given to charity.

Then she turned her attention to his closet.

A single dress shirt and a nearly ancient black suit hung alone on the pole inside of it. His funeral suit, her father had called it. Appropriately enough because funerals were the sole occasions for which he'd worn it.

In fact, funerals were the only events he'd attended. Everything else—holidays, christenings, parties, weddings, even church on Sundays were a waste of his time, he'd said, and had refused flatly to do anything about them.

Ivey took the shirt, suit coat and pants off the hangers, folded them and set them in one of the charity boxes.

The closet's top shelf held only an extra pillow and blanket, so she left it as it was, and set her sights on the floor.

There were four pairs of shoes there—two pairs of work boots, one pair of cowboy boots, and a pair of black dress shoes to go with his funeral clothes. They all joined the charity boxes, too.

And that left the stacks and stacks of paperback books that occupied the other half of the closet floor.

The books had been Silas's single indulgence. They were all westerns—something Ivey had never realized before because she hadn't paid any attention to what he'd read. She and Savannah had just known that disturbing his reading ran the risk of raising his wrath.

She went for more boxes for the books, thinking she'd donate them to the library, and it was as she was transferring them from the closet floor that something fell out of one of them, drifting back into the closet as if it didn't want to be taken from its longtime resting place.

Ivey knelt down and leaned in to retrieve it, surprised to discover it was a photograph.

Very surprised.

And not just because Silas had never taken pictures of her or Savannah, never so much as let them buy the ones taken at school. But because this photograph was of her mother.

Ivey didn't recognize her instantly and instead glanced at it wondering what Silas was doing with a picture of some woman in a wedding dress. Then it dawned on her who the woman was.

Neither Ivey nor Savannah remembered their mother on their own. Savannah had only been four years old and Ivey had been just past her first birthday when Eileen Heller had telephoned her sister-in-law across the road, asked if the other woman would watch Ivey and Savannah while she ran some errands, brought them to the larger Heller house and then left town with a farm equipment salesman.

That had been the last anyone had seen of her. Or heard from her. And after that Silas had destroyed—or at least claimed to have destroyed—any pictures there had ever been of his wife.

Ivey and Savannah had seen a few anyway. Eileen Heller appeared in some family photos the other branch of the Heller clan had, so after a moment of looking at the wedding portrait Ivey recognized the delicate features staring out from the white halolike veil. Smiling Savannah's smile. Looking for all the world as if she were a happy bride.

Ivey had always wondered about that. About why her mother had ever married Silas in the first place. Because if her father had forever been the man she'd known, she couldn't understand it.

He must have put on a good front until after the wedding, was the explanation she'd always given herself. And then, when his true colors had presented themselves, that's what had driven her mother away.

But looking at that photograph that her father had hidden away, Ivey imagined him secretly peering at it in the privacy of his room, feeling the pain of having been betrayed, and something else occurred to her for the first time. Something that should have occurred to her long ago, except that she'd been mired in her own dealings with her father and had let that color her opinion.

Maybe Silas hadn't always been the man she and Savannah had known. Maybe he'd been different before her mother had left. Maybe her mother's leaving had been what had turned Silas so sour.

It seemed possible. Even likely. In fact, it suddenly seemed very likely that what had turned him into that cold, remote, shell of a man had been her mother's leaving.

"I'll bet he heard bells and whistles over you," Ivey muttered to herself in sudden revelation.

And just as suddenly she felt a wave of forgiveness for the man. For how rough he'd made her and Savannah's growing-up years. It couldn't have been easy for him to rear two daughters on his own, two constant reminders that the woman he'd loved had left him.

Was that how Cully felt when he looked at Amy and Randa? Ivey wondered.

If he did, he hid it well. She hadn't seen any sign of it at all.

Yet surely there must be times when those little girls reminded him of his ex-wife.

Was he so much better than her own father had been at not taking it out on them?

He had to be because those two kids were crazy about him.

And so are you, a little voice whispered in the back of her mind.

Was she crazy about Cully?

Ivey gave that some serious thought.

She liked him. A lot.

She enjoyed his company. He made her laugh. She had fun when she was with him. She hated it when he left and couldn't wait until they could be together again. And in between, her thoughts wandered to him almost constantly.

That definitely sounded as if it qualified as being crazy about him.

And that realization unnerved her.

What did she really know about Cully Culhane after all these years? she asked herself as she stayed sitting on her heels, half in, half out of the closet.

She knew he'd been a hell-raiser as a teenager. She knew he'd been a heartbreaker. She knew he'd been a good athlete and had graduated valedictorian but shunned college in order to stay in Elk Creek and work his family's ranch.

But she didn't know much about the man he'd become.

Sure she knew surface things. He was a father. He and his brothers had apparently made an even greater success of the family's ranch than it had been all those years ago. He was a recent—*very* recent—addition to the legion of divorced men.

But none of those surface things were a basis for forming any kind of real judgment about him.

And if she'd learned anything from the fiasco with Arlen, it was to look beyond the surface to find what the man himself was. And to do it *before* she let herself get crazy about him.

"Easier said than done," she muttered out loud.

Especially when being with Cully had such a strong tendency to wipe her mind blank while only her senses ruled. That was not likely to improve her judgment.

"So you're treading on thin ice," she warned.

Thinner ice than she'd treaded on even with Arlen, because the intensity of her attraction to Cully was so much more powerful, so much more all-encompassing. So much more blinding.

A wise woman wouldn't venture out onto thin ice, that little voice of caution in her head pointed out as she set the picture of her mother aside and went on putting her father's books in the box—shaking each one out first in case anything else was lurking within the pages.

But the only way to avoid the thin ice was to avoid Cully. To not see him again.

She thought seriously about that, too.

The last thing a person with poor judgment in men should do was indulge in time with a man whose appeal was so potent it could cloud the judgment of Solomon, if Solomon had been a woman.

But no matter how forcefully she told herself that not seeing Cully was what she should do, it didn't matter. Just the idea of it was as unfathomable as the idea of not breathing.

How had it come this far this fast? she asked herself, surprised to find that it had.

She didn't know.

But if she couldn't stop it, stop herself, then she knew she'd better at least proceed with all the caution thin ice called for. She'd better step carefully and keep her eyes and ears open.

But would it matter? Was her judgment of men so askew that she wasn't even capable of telling the good guys from the bad ones?

She didn't know that, either.

The best she could hope for was to try to maintain some perspective and learn from her time with Cully, concentrate on honing her judgment skills.

Because what she *couldn't* do was deny herself this time with him.

"So just be careful," she said, sounding like Savannah might if her sister were there to talk this over with.

And she would be careful, she vowed. She'd be very, very careful.

She just hoped it was possible in view of the fact that Cully's reputation from high school was well-deserved—a woman hadn't really been kissed until she'd been kissed by him.

And once she had, it was next to impossible not to be crazy about him....

Ivey hadn't been on a nighttime picnic since she was a teenager in Elk Creek. And even then they hadn't really been private picnics. In a small town where entertainments were at a premium, it was a common Friday and Saturday night occurrence for bonfires to be built out in the middle of nowhere for teens to gather around, cooking hot dogs on the ends of sticks and roasting marshmallows, and drinking an illicit beer here and there.

But a boy-girl picnic alone? That hadn't been something the town's biggest tomboy had been invited on.

Still, having spent her fair share at the communal-type picnics, Ivey knew just how to dress for riding horseback around her property and ending up fireside for a supper out in the open with Cully that evening.

She wore a red cable-knit sweater over a button-down collar shirt, her most comfortable pair of blue jeans and—in lieu of cowboy boots—tennis shoes over two pairs of socks.

She left her hair loose and curly around her face, neck and shoulders, applied only enough makeup to accentuate her eyes and hide her freckles, and added a few drops of perfume to her wrists—telling herself as she did that it wasn't for Cully's sake but for her own to counteract the scent of the horses.

As four o'clock drew near she took a wool jacket from her closet, tying it around her waist as she went downstairs. The nights weren't winter cold yet so she doubted she'd need the jacket, but just in case the bonfire wasn't enough to chase away the chill once the sun went down, she'd have it.

She knew Cully was likely to come in the back way as he did when he was tending his animals in her barn, so she locked the front door and went into the kitchen to watch for him through the window over the sink, trying the whole time to curb the anticipation that was growing inside her as she counted the minutes until she'd get to see him again.

She didn't have to count many of them before she spotted him riding in from the direction of his place, sitting atop a big gray stallion and leading a smaller brown mare for her.

He sat in the saddle as if he were born to it, tall, straight-backed, rolling easily with each sway of the animal's steps.

He wore his usual cowboy boots and blue jeans be-

neath a sky blue flannel shirt that let the white henley
he had on underneath it show at his throat and around
his forearms where the flannel sleeves were rolled to
his elbows.

The planes of his cheeks were clean shaven and his
sable-colored hair shimmered in the late-day sunshine.

She literally had a physical reaction to that first sight
of him. A shiver of excitement climbed her spine and
left her whole body atingle. He couldn't ride in fast
enough for her taste, and without thinking that she
might seem too anxious, she rushed out to the back
stoop just as he walked the horse up to the rear of the
house.

"Am I late?" he asked by way of greeting.

Clearly her eagerness had given the impression that
she was in a hurry so Ivey forced herself to sound
nonchalant to amend it. "No, I just saw you coming,"
she said as if her heart weren't racing and seeing him
wasn't the highlight of her day.

"I packed some food," she said then. "It's in the
fridge."

"Leave it," he answered, patting one side of the
saddlebags that draped the horse's haunches. "This
was my idea, my treat."

"Shall we just go then?"

"We'd better. Don't want to waste what little day-
light we have left."

He swung down from his horse in one graceful
sweep of his big body and pulled the reins forward over
the animal's head to dangle to the ground as he held
out a hand to her. "Come on and let me help you up.
You've been away so long that we have to count you
as a city girl by now," he said with a hint of teasing
in his voice and a gleam of it in the ice blue eyes that

seemed like reflections of his shirt on a cool, glassy pond.

"I haven't been away *that* long," she countered as she pulled her back door closed behind her and met Cully alongside the mare.

She didn't wait for his help in mounting but he grasped her around the waist anyway, half lifting her as if she were weightless. Through two layers of clothing it could hardly count as intimate contact and yet it was enough to send warm feelings sluicing all through her.

In order to keep her mind off the sensation, once she was seated she said, "Where are the girls for tonight? I thought you might bring them."

"They're at a friend's house for a sleepover," Cully answered as he got back on his horse. "Were you hoping for chaperons?" he asked with an ornery crook to his smile.

"Do I need chaperons?" she bantered back.

"Maybe," he said, arching one eyebrow. "But it's too late now."

He reined his horse to face the way he'd come and got down to business. "I thought we'd start along the border of our place and yours. Then we can work our way around, build our bonfire over near the lake on the south side."

"Okay," Ivey agreed, urging her horse in the same direction his was headed.

They rode side by side from there, away from the house and barn and out into the open countryside. As they came upon the fields and pastures he and his brothers leased from Ivey and Savannah, Cully kept up a running description of what they were doing with the land.

On some of it they were growing feed corn, wheat and hay that was already baled for the season and stacked in small piles waiting to be picked up and taken where it would be most needed during the long winter months.

Beyond the sections the Culhanes were farming were those they used to graze portions of their herd of beef cows and some of the horses they bred. Of course the main herds were pastured on their own land, as well as more of their own land being used for the farming, but Cully explained that they'd expanded so extensively in the time since he, Clint and Yance had taken over from their folks that they'd decided it would be more cost-effective to buy the Heller place outright rather than go on leasing it.

Ivey listened as attentively as she could, all the while taking in the view of the land she hadn't been out on in fifteen years. Her thoughts kept being invaded by memories of the times before that, working under her father's heavy hand in those same fields and pastures.

But even more often she was distracted by the view of Cully himself. By the pure potency of his presence. The sight of his handsome profile against the setting sun. His straight, broad back narrowing to hips that were cradled in his saddle. The spread of massive, muscular thighs around the horse's sides. The vision of his long arms stretching out, his thick, blunt fingers pointing to what he was talking about.

It all made it difficult to think about grain yield and calfing and crop rotation. But Ivey did her best.

They reached the small lake on the southwest side of the ranch as the sun disappeared behind the Rocky Mountains and left the sky a bright persimmon and pumpkin explosion of color.

With just enough light left to gather wood for their bonfire they tied their horses to the branches of one of the fir trees that formed a semicircle around half the lake. Once they had enough sticks, dry branches of pine needles and several logs Cully cut with an ax from his saddlebags, they chose a spot near the shore of the clear, still water and built their fire.

As they did, Cully wrapped up what he'd been talking about since leaving her house. "So, there you have it," he said. "What we've been doing with this place and what we'd like to do with it in the future."

"It all sounds good. I'm impressed," she said, although she didn't tell him she was more impressed by him than by anything else. "It looks like you're finally doing all the things that could have made this place a bigger success if my father had taken my uncle's advice years and years ago."

"Why didn't he?"

"Stubbornness, I guess. My father was determined to do things *his* way. Part of that meant not hiring ranch hands because then he wouldn't be self-reliant. So instead he was bent on working this place with only the help of two daughters who were supposed to have been sons."

"And who were just kids in the bargain."

"That, too. We weren't the kind of manpower necessary to handle a spread this size."

Cully nodded his agreement as he snapped open a blanket and set it on the ground near the fire. "You didn't have much fun growing up around here, did you?"

Ivey laughed. "Not much, no."

Cully set his saddlebags on the blanket and gestured for her to sit down. Ivey did, sitting Indian fashion, angled toward their bonfire but not so much that Cully couldn't sit facing her. Which he did.

From the saddlebags he took a thermos that broke down into the canister and two cups he filled with steaming coffee. Then out came several sandwiches, a container of potato salad and another of pickles and olives.

Ivey would rather have cooked hot dogs on the end of sticks—what she'd packed for their dinner—but didn't end up too disappointed when she saw him pull out a bag of marshmallows.

He served her a sandwich that was chock-full of various lunch meats, lettuce, tomatoes and cheese, and handed her a fork to eat out of the communal potato salad carton he put between them.

Then he said, "I'm surprised you and Savannah didn't sell this place right away after old Silas passed on. I'm glad you didn't—no way we could have bought it then—but surprised just the same."

"It's funny, isn't it?" she agreed. "But we never even talked about it. Our uncle Shag took over what there was of the place that was working at the time. He paid the taxes from selling the crops that first year, and a few animals every year after that until you guys wanted to lease the land. When that happened he called us and advised us to do it and we've paid the taxes out of that money ever since. But we never thought about actually selling out."

"Maybe you have deeper roots here than you realized," Cully suggested between bites of his food.

Ivey thought about that while she tasted the potato salad, not minding that they were sharing it. In fact she liked the quiet intimacy that was there between them and that just seemed to seal it.

"I don't think either Savannah or I have ever considered that we might have roots here at all," she said after thinking about his comment.

"But this is where you ran to when you hit a rough patch in the life you made for yourself in Cheyenne," he reminded.

She couldn't deny that. "It has felt good to be back again." Although she really didn't know if it would have felt as good without Cully being around, the way Savannah had insinuated. "I even managed to finally go through my father's things today—we never did that when he died."

"Was it hard on you?"

"No, not hard. But it did give me a different image of him," she said, going on to explain finding the picture of her mother and all it had made her think about.

"I couldn't help wondering," she said when she'd finished, "if Savannah and I reminded him of what he'd lost. If that was at least a portion of why he seemed to resent us so much. Do your girls remind you of their mother?"

"Sometimes," Cully admitted. "But I don't resent them for it."

"How about their being girls?" Ivey went on testing, wanting to know more about Cully's feelings about his daughters, thinking that it was a way to judge him as a man. "Do you wish they were boys?"

He laughed, a full, rich, easy rumble of a sound. "I worry about 'em bein' girls. My brothers and I did an awful lot of playin' with the females around here and no randy bucks better try any of it with my daughters or they'll have hell to pay. In that respect it'd be easier on me if they were boys. On the other hand," he added with another chuckle, "my havin' girls is probably payback for foolin' around so much with other men's daughters. But no, I've never wished Amy and Randa were anything but what they are.''

For a few moments they ate and stared at the blaze, listening to the crackle of the pine needles.

Then Cully said, ''I guess it's no wonder you and Savannah hightailed it away from home as soon as you could.''

''Well, Savannah could have left earlier. She put off going because of me. And because of Clint.''

Cully nodded. ''But she didn't waste any time when you were finally through with school.''

Ivey conceded the truth in that.

''What would have happened if your old...father had passed on before you left? Would the two of you have stayed here?''

''I don't know,'' Ivey admitted with another small laugh.

''Doesn't seem like either of you had a wandering spirit—four years of college together and then staying in that same apartment you moved into when you graduated all those years ago. Seems more like you just wanted to get away from Silas.''

''We definitely wanted that.''

''I'd hate like hell for that to be the case with my girls.''

''Somehow for my father, I think our leaving was just a relief.''

They'd finished eating by then and stuffed all but the marshmallows back in the saddlebags. Cully tossed the leather satchel aside and borrowed a long stick from the pile he'd been using to feed the fire. He set it across his widespread thighs as he tore open the marshmallow bag.

Maybe it was the bringing out of the marshmallows, but somehow Ivey had the urge to lighten the tone of things. She gave Cully a sideways glance as he jabbed two of the fluffy white concoctions onto the stick and teased, "So you did some things with other men's daughters that you don't want done to your own, huh?"

His wonderful mouth stretched into a lazy grin. "One or two. But not without the daughters' full consent." He held the marshmallows just close enough to the flames for them to catch the heat. "What about you? You do anything you wouldn't want your daddy to know about?"

Ivey laughed yet again. "You must not remember me too well. I told you, I never so much as had a date or went to a school dance."

"How about once you got off on your own? In college? After college?"

"You mean was I led astray in the big city?" she joked.

It was his turn to give her the sideways glance. "Were you?"

"Maybe once or twice," she rephrased his own answer, wanting to sound more worldly than she was. But then she couldn't go through with it and said, "Well, once anyway."

Cully raised his eyebrows and looked straight at her. "Just once?"

"Not just one time. I meant just one man—Arlen. And only after we were engaged..." She could feel heat rising in her cheeks but she wasn't sure if it was due to talking about something so personal or because she was admitting to being relatively inexperienced in the ways of love. "I guess that doesn't really count as being led astray after all," she amended.

He was watching her with a knowing, amused expression on that handsome face that was gilded by the fire's glow and it made her uneasy. To divert his attention to something else she nodded at the marshmallow. "Aren't those about ready?"

He went on staring at her a moment longer, as if he could see through her but liked what he saw. Then he checked the marshmallows.

They were a golden brown and he aimed the one on the end of the stick her way so she could take it, still seeming more intent on her.

Ivey plucked the marshmallow as if it were a flower and popped the whole thing in her mouth.

That left the second one for Cully but he took his time eating it, all the while watching her.

He seemed to be enjoying how unnerved he could make her and she decided to accept it as a challenge and met him eye to eye.

Not a good choice.

Just as she looked at him he'd finished his marshmallow and was sucking the last of the sticky goo off his thumb and then his forefinger.

She didn't know why it was one of the most sensual things she'd ever seen, but it was. Unconsciously, naturally sensual, as his gaze still focused on her. And she couldn't help wondering if the sexiness of that gesture was just the outward sign of what was going through his mind.

He eased into a lazy smile and reached over to press his now clean thumb to her top lip, cupping her chin with the rest of his hand and drawing that thumb downward.

Maybe she'd had a morsel of marshmallow on her mouth because she tasted sweetness when his thumb brushed across the sensitive inside of her bottom lip. But by then she was so drawn to the pure magnetism of him, to the feel of that big, gentle hand tilting her face toward him, that it didn't matter that she might have had a speck of something there.

He leaned forward and replaced his thumb with his lips on hers in a kiss that was soft, tender. A kiss that slowly deepened as his hand slid to the back of her head to pull her closer, as his mouth opened over hers, as his tongue came courting.

Ivey lost herself in that kiss as it grew hotter, more intense. He urged her backward, laying her on the blanket as he stretched his big, lean body beside hers, his other hand caressing her cheek as he worked an expert magic on her mouth.

She matched his tongue thrust for thrust with her own; her lips parted every bit as far as his, seeking, exploring. Their hunger for one another burned hotter, brighter, with each passing moment.

Ivey's arms were around him, her hands splayed against the hard expanse of his back, and all she could think about was how badly she wanted to be doing more than kissing him. How badly she wanted to feel his touch not just on her face, but on every inch of her body. How badly she wanted to be free of all the layers of clothes that kept them apart, to feel his weight not just beside her but on top of her...

But just then Cully stopped kissing her altogether.

He pressed his forehead to hers, took a ragged breath and sighed it out.

"This isn't a good idea," he said in a husky tone.

"No, it probably isn't," she agreed, her own voice soft and as breathless as she felt.

"I'm out of control with you," he confessed, not sounding pleased about it.

"I know the feeling." Thin ice. She was definitely on thin ice. And not being cautious about it the way she'd vowed she would be.

Cully pushed himself into a sitting position, took her hand and helped her up, too. "You'd think we were a couple of hormonal teenagers."

"But we're not."

"Tell my body that."

She was working too hard at convincing her own.

Cully reached a hand to the side of her face again, laying his warm palm to her cheek, following the crest of her cheekbone with that same thumb that had started this whole thing in the first place, rubbing back and forth, back and forth in a gentle massage that felt so good it was almost hypnotizing.

"I want to be careful here, Ivey," he confided. "I'm just havin' a tough time of it. You're in my blood."

"Like a virus."

He laughed. "No, not like a virus. Like a great shot of bourbon that lights fire to my insides and leaves me feelin' too good to think straight."

Ivey nodded. It was a description she could identify with because being near him did the same thing to her. "So what are we going to do about it?"

He shook his head, still caressing her face as if he couldn't bear not to touch her, holding her eyes with his pale ones. "For right now what I've done about it is stopped kissin' you while I still could. But I can't promise what'll happen any other time."

"Maybe we shouldn't see each other," she suggested in an almost inaudible voice because the idea was so hard to even entertain.

"Maybe we shouldn't. But I don't think I can stay away, either. Unless you want me to."

"No, I don't want you to," she said in a hurry.

"Then I guess we're just going to have to take things as they come."

She nodded, this time with only a bare raising of her chin.

"And for now, we better call it a night because if I sit on this blanket in front of this fire with you for another minute, there isn't any way I'm not goin' right back to what we were doin' just now."

He didn't wait for her to agree or disagree with that, but slid his hand away from her face and got to his feet.

While Ivey gathered up the sack of marshmallows to stuff back into his saddlebag and stood, too, he kicked enough dirt onto the fire to put it out. Once he had, he snatched up the blanket, folding it into a tight square.

One last check to make sure the fire was completely out and then they crossed the few feet to where the animals waited patiently.

Cully draped his saddlebags over his shoulder to free his hands and stuffed the blanket into a satchel that was still across the back end of Ivey's horse. Then he helped her mount the mare, much the way he had before, although this time Ivey thought he took his hands away from her waist quicker, as if to let them linger might set off more of what they were both trying to avoid.

He untied her reins and handed them up to her, then turned to his own horse, refitting his saddlebags to the rear of the saddle.

Ivey watched him, feasting on the view, still wanting

him, wanting to be in his arms, even as he slipped a booted foot into the stirrup and rose up with more of that unconscious grace that made it a sight to behold.

They rode the short distance back to her house without saying anything and only as they drew near her door did she cool off enough to realize the air was actually quite chilly.

They stopped a scant few feet from the concrete stoop, dismounted and went up the steps. That was when she realized that her evening with him was ending and she was struck by the usual reluctance to see him go. She knew it wouldn't be wise to ask him in, to prolong their time together when passion was waiting so near the surface to be reignited, but she was also much too aware of the fact that she didn't know when she might see him again after this.

"Would you and your girls like to come to dinner tomorrow night?" she heard herself say almost the moment the idea occurred to her. "I've been feeling like doing a little cooking and it's always better if it's for more than one."

"Or two," he said knowingly, obviously realizing she'd included his daughters as the chaperons he'd teased her about wanting along tonight.

"Unless you're busy," she added to give him an excuse if he didn't want to come.

"I'm not busy," he assured.

Milky moonlight reflected from the side of the house, making it brighter than it had seemed on the ride in and illuminating them both as Cully stared down into her face again, studying it, smiling a secret sort of smile.

"About six? Would that be okay?" she asked in yet another hurry because she was so unnerved by his ap-

praisal, by that smile, by the desire to slide her arms
around his waist and lay her head against his broad
chest....

"Six," he repeated.

Then he kissed her again. Not a soft, chaste kiss, but
not a passion-inflamed one like they'd shared out on
the blanket, either. This was somewhere in between the
two—familiar, warm, openmouthed, with the passion
only a hint around the edges.

Still, it was enough to make Ivey's knees go weak
and she reconsidered inviting him in after all.

But then he ended that kiss, too, and stepped away
from her.

"Tomorrow night at six," he said.

"Right."

"With Amy and Randa."

"With Amy and Randa."

"I'll be lookin' forward to it."

Me, too, she thought, but she didn't say it.

Instead she watched him back down the steps and
reach for the reins to both animals without taking his
eyes off her, as if he didn't want to lose sight of her.

"'Night," she called as he got on his horse.

"Sleep tight," he answered, finally reining the animals around and urging them into a fast canter to take
him home.

Ivey stayed on the stoop for as long as she could see
him riding off into the dark. She couldn't help wishing
that he hadn't left at all. That he was going inside with
her right that minute.

Inside.

Upstairs.

To her bed.

To do things she wouldn't have wanted her father to know about.

Things old Silas probably wouldn't have approved of.

But things she wanted to do just the same.

With Cully Culhane.

Oh, yeah, she was definitely on thin ice....

Chapter Seven

Ivey spent the next morning shopping in town. Her plan was just for grocery shopping for the foodstuffs she needed to make dinner for Cully and his daughters, but as she walked past the maternity and baby shop—which also sold clothing for small children—a window display caught her eye and she ended up buying more than groceries and a bottle of wine to go with supper.

At noon she met Della, Kansas, Beth and Jackson's new wife, Ally, at Margie Wilson's Café for lunch, girltalk, and encouragement for her to stay in Elk Creek permanently. She didn't give any answer one way or another about that but she did listen raptly when she managed to turn the conversation to talk about Cully's ex-wife and kids.

The other women confirmed Cully's description of his wife as flighty and commitment-shy, as a woman who was free with promises to donate to a bake sale or help out with a church project but never managed to actually follow through with anything.

And they joked about the fact that for all the womanizing Cully Culhane—and his brothers, too, for that matter—had done in their youth, not one of the three of them seemed to know what to do with the two little girls Cully's wife had left behind. Poor Amy and Randa, they agreed, never got to go to parties or church services without their hair sticking out every which way, wearing jeans and flannel shirts and looking like two little boys.

Ivey didn't tell them that she had a remedy for that in the gaily wrapped packages beside her chair.

The afternoon hours were filled with baking a cake and preparing for dinner before Ivey took her second shower of the day, washed her hair and dressed in a V-neck tunic that reached nearly to the knees of a pair of identically colored purple leggings. She left her hair in its natural riot of curls and applied only light makeup.

She was back downstairs with about twenty minutes to spare—just enough time to set the table. As she did a loud knock on the front door startled her.

She hadn't expected Cully to be early. But it pleased her just the same to think that he was so anxious to see her that he couldn't wait until six.

"Coming, coming, coming," she chanted to herself as she nearly skipped down the hallway alongside the stairs to answer more insistent pounding.

But standing on her front porch when she opened the door was not Cully, Amy or Randa.

"Arlen!"

"Don't look so surprised. It's not like I'm back from the dead," he said sarcastically.

Her former fiancé was dressed in brown slacks and a brown argyle sweater over a white shirt. As always, not a single strand of his dusty brown hair was out of place and he looked like a rich college boy on his way to his fraternity house. But not for anything pleasant because his pointy, refined features were set in a cold, hard expression.

He didn't wait to be invited in. Instead he yanked the screen wide and came inside so forcefully Ivey had to step quickly out of the way or be shoved. And like a gust of wind in his wake, his anger blew at her, suffusing her with a sense of fear.

She'd never been afraid of Arlen before. For all his criticisms and put-downs, he hadn't seemed menacing. But then she hadn't ever seen him as angry as he seemed to be at her at that moment.

And somehow she couldn't help wondering if this was yet another level of the man that she hadn't realized existed. A level that she would have reached in time. A level that made her feel as if she were in some kind of danger from him....

"What are you doing here?" she asked as calmly as she could, leaving the door open to follow him into her living room.

He didn't answer her. He merely glanced around, an expression of disgust forming on his face at what he saw. "So this is where you're *living* now. And I thought that apartment was shabby."

"My apartment is small, it isn't shabby. And this is an old house," she said, regretting that she'd even dignified the snide comment with a response.

"This is old, all right," he agreed with a sneer. "An old hovel. No wonder you don't have any class, look where you came from. And what you've run back to—

right where you belong—in hicksville with the rest of the bumpkins.''

Ivey didn't address that. She just reiterated her previous question. "Why are you here, Arlen?''

He glared at her with so much hatred in his face it twisted the usually handsome visage into an ugly mask. ''The engagement ring cost me five *thousand* dollars. Did you think I was just going to let you keep it?''

Ah, the engagement ring. She'd still had it on her finger when she'd arrived back in Elk Creek on Saturday. She'd been thinking about so many other things, it hadn't occurred to her to take it off before that.

But she'd removed it the moment she'd realized she was still wearing it. Then she'd retrieved its velvet box from the apartment in Cheyenne when she'd brought her other things home two days ago so it would have a safe nesting place while she debated with herself about whether she should return it by insured mail or if the more honorable thing was to give it back in person.

''I have it ready for you,'' she said, hurrying to the rolltop desk that occupied the alcove in the corner of the room. She'd put the velvet box in one of the desk drawers and now wasted no time getting it out. She had every intention of handing it over to Arlen while still keeping as much distance from him as she could, even as she told herself she was being silly.

Of course he was angry. He had every right to be. That didn't make him dangerous.

But she just couldn't shake that sense of fear.

And it didn't help that when she turned from the desk he was standing right there, not a foot behind her, so near that she almost bumped into him.

"Oh...uh, here you are," she said lamely, wishing she didn't sound as uneasy as she felt.

"Do you have any idea how much you embarrassed me?" he asked, his voice low and ominous, coming through clenched teeth.

"I think I do, yes. And I'm sorry for it. I told you that on the phone."

"*I told you that on the phone,*" he repeated, mocking her. "Like that makes a difference. You're *sorry* for it. Big deal. All week long I've had to answer questions about what you did, why you did it. I've been to work every day, hearing people snicker behind my back, thinking you had some reason for not marrying me, like it was *my* fault. All week long..." His voice was almost a feral growl, like a vicious animal unleashed.

Ivey's grip around the ring box was so tight her nails dug into her palm. She forced her fist open so she could hold the box out to him, hoping he'd take it and go. "Here's the ring, Arlen."

He snatched it away as if she might not relinquish it after all, and jammed it into his pants pocket. But he didn't budge from that spot that had her trapped in the alcove, blocking her only exit.

"You're so stupid," he nearly hissed. "I always thought you were short on brains but I never knew just what an ignorant witch you are."

She had a flash of memory right then, of her father ranting and raving and calling her and Savannah names, here in this very house. And suddenly Ivey felt disoriented, as if the past and present were mingling.

Then things came into focus again. This wasn't her father. She wasn't a helpless child. And she didn't have to stand there and accept this treatment from Arlen or anyone else, no matter how many weddings she'd run out on.

"I'd like you to leave now, Arlen."

"I'll leave when I'm good and ready. Just the way you left when you were. With me standing at the altar, in front of everybody I know, making a fool of me."

She tried to edge around him to get out of that claustrophobic space but he stood with one arm stretched across the entry arch to the side wall, completely barring her exit. Then, as if even that might not be enough to keep her where he wanted her, he grabbed her upper arm in a punishing grip of his other hand. A grip so tight pain shot clear through her elbow and down into her wrist.

"You never were good enough for me," he said, shaking her, his voice louder but no less enraged. "I was doing you a favor. You, a stupid *kindergarten* teacher. A glorified baby-sitter, that's all you are. That's all you're good for. You know what they say about teachers—"

"I know that it's time for you to leave," she said firmly.

"I thought I might be able to mold you into something better than you are. Something at least presentable. Something with some class. But I see now that I was kidding myself. You'd have embarrassed me all the way down the line. My bumpkin wife. I'd have been ashamed to take you out in public!" He was shouting now and spittle shot from his mouth.

Ivey tried to pull her arm free of his grasp but he only tightened it.

"You're hurting me, Arlen," she said in a voice none too low herself.

"Serves you right," he countered, tightening it all

the more as he stared fiercely down into her face. "You're not even that pretty. I don't know what I ever saw in you. No brains, no looks, no personality—that's you. You should have gotten down on your knees and kissed the ground I walk on for even giving you a second look. Maybe that's where you belong now—on your knees—"

"I don't think so," came a voice from behind Arlen. The deep, deep voice of Cully.

Still Arlen didn't loosen his hold, even as he looked over his shoulder at the other man who had come silently into the house and stood just behind him.

"Who are you?" Arlen snarled.

"Doesn't matter who I am," Cully answered reasonably, calmly, but giving no quarter just the same. "Let her go."

"This is none of your business," Arlen said loudly.

"You're wrong there. Let her go."

"Go to hell."

From around Arlen, Ivey could see Cully shake his head slowly, as if it were just too bad the other man hadn't taken his advice. Then his own hand shot out with lightning quickness to grab the arm Arlen had stretched across the alcove's entry and twist it behind his back, pulling up hard and fast, surprising him.

"Let her go," Cully repeated, his tone part warning, part threat.

Arlen didn't do as he was told immediately and that hesitation made Cully wrench his arm higher still, yanking Arlen half out of the alcove's entrance and causing enough pain this time for Arlen to involuntarily release his hold on Ivey.

Ivey wasted no time in getting out of harm's way, nearly lunging into the living room.

"Are you all right?" Cully asked with a concerned frown aimed in her direction.

"Yes. Now."

"Did you invite this guy here?"

"No, I didn't."

"You have any reason you want him to hang around?"

"No," she said, shivering suddenly at what had just passed, at thoughts of what might have happened had Cully not arrived when he had.

Cully turned his gaze back on Arlen. "Want to leave under your own steam or shall I help you to that fancy sports car out front?"

"Just get your hammy hand off me," Arlen growled.

"Guess you need some help."

Cully kept his hold of the smaller man's arm and used it to steer him in the direction of the door.

"You want her?" Arlen demanded in a near shriek along the way. "You can have her. You and every other bumpkin here in Dogpatch!"

Cully pushed the screen door open with Arlen's body and shoved him out onto the porch. Then, as Ivey watched through the picture window, he escorted her former fiancé all the way to the driver's side of Arlen's pride-and-joy Porsche. Once they were there Cully opened that door for him and gave him no small amount of encouragement to get in.

Finally free of Cully's grip and safely ensconced in his car, Arlen turned his insults and abuse on Cully in a voice that carried all the way inside the house. Until Cully took a single step nearer the driver's-side door, then Arlen started the engine in a hurry and drove off, leaving a trail of dust and gravel spewing from his tires.

Cully stayed standing where he was, keeping an eye

on the retreating sports car until it had turned onto the main road and squealed off out of sight.

Little by little Ivey came back to herself, realizing Arlen really was gone. That what had happened with him was over. That she was safe.

That was when her focus broadened enough to take in Amy and Randa in the cab of Cully's truck, parked not far from where Arlen's car had been.

The two tiny girls were on their knees on the truck seat, staring with wide eyes and mouths agape at their father.

Long, confident strides took Cully over to the truck then, where he opened the passenger's door and said something to his kids. But he still left them there and came back inside alone.

"Are you sure you're okay?" he asked Ivey when he joined her in the living room where she stood at the picture window.

She nodded. "You came in the nick of time," she said, ignoring the lingering ache in her arm where Arlen had surely left bruises.

"Would you rather not do this dinner tonight? We don't have to, you know. Maybe you're not up to it."

"No, no, you guys are just what the doctor ordered," she assured quickly, meaning every word of it. Not only had she looked forward to this evening with Cully, with his daughters, but the last thing she wanted at that moment was to be left by herself. "Please, bring Amy and Randa in. Let's try to forget about this whole thing."

Cully studied her as if to make certain she knew what she was saying.

"Honestly," she added. "Go get the girls. Dinner is almost ready."

He assented with raised eyebrows but an expression that said he wasn't completely convinced she was as okay as she was pretending to be. Still, he turned on his heel and went back out to the truck.

Ivey managed to get her wobbly legs to take her to the door so she could hold open the screen and welcome her guests the way she should have in the beginning.

As Cully lifted Amy and Randa down from the truck they were full of questions.

"Was that a bad man?" Ivey heard Amy ask, obviously referring to Arlen.

"He used'd bad words," Randa observed as if someone might deny it otherwise. "Is that how come you weren't bein' friendly to 'im?"

"Yeah, you pushed 'im. You told us not never to push people, but you did it," Amy went on before her father had a chance to say anything.

"And you made 'im get in his car," Randa chimed in excitedly. "I don't think he wanted to get in his car and go 'way."

"The man was not being nice to Ivey so I made him leave and that's all there was to it," Cully finally managed to say on the way up the porch steps.

"He looked'd mad," Randa offered.

"He looked'd *mean!*" Amy amended, drawing the last word out for emphasis.

"Hi, girls," Ivey interrupted, hoping to distract them as they crossed the porch to the door.

But it only served to redirect their questions to her instead of to their father.

"Did you know that mean man?" Randa asked.

"Daddy made us stay in the truck 'cuz we could see

you through the window and he said he din't like the looks of what was goin' on,'' Amy explained.

"And then we hear'd that mean man yellin' at you and—''

"Okay, girls, enough,'' Cully said. "It's all over with. Let's talk about something else.''

"Why don't you guys come in?'' Ivey suggested because the two little girls had stalled at the entrance.

They were dressed the way they had been before—denim coveralls, this time over plaid flannel shirts—and their hair was still a jumble of chopped-off angles. But one of them spotted the beribboned packages on the coffee table in the living room and that helped get them across the threshold as they both made a beeline in that direction to give rapt attention to the Sesame Street wrapping paper.

It freed Cully to come in, too, close the door behind him and take yet another lengthy look at Ivey.

"Hi,'' she said with a wry little laugh, as if they were just now setting eyes on each other.

She drank in the sight of him in his jeans and navy blue western shirt and wanted very, very badly to slip into his strong arms, to press her head to his solid chest and have him hold her. Tight. Until all the jitters, all the uneasiness, all the fear of her encounter with Arlen could be washed away in the warm reassurance of Cully's big body.

But of course she couldn't do that and had to settle for the warmth of his gaze instead. Even though it came from beneath a brow still furrowed with concern.

Amy and Randa, however, were not going to let them idle in the entryway. Not with the temptation of two gifts right there in front of them.

"What're these?'' Randa asked.

"Do you gots some kids that these are their birfday presents?" Amy chimed in with more of an attempt at subtlety.

Before Ivey answered either question she said in an aside to Cully, "I hope you don't mind—" In fact she hoped it a lot because she was slightly worried about how he might view the gifts. "I was in town today and saw these outfits in the window of the kids' store. They made me think of Amy and Randa and…well, I just bought them."

Before he had a chance to say anything, she led the way into the living room, seizing his daughters' excitement as an escape from the effects of Arlen's visit.

Cully followed as she said to the girls, "They're presents for you two."

"Can we open 'em?" Randa asked.

"It's okay with me if it's okay with your dad."

Cully gave the go-ahead with a lifting of his chin and his daughters tore into the wrapping in a frenzy.

While they did Ivey hoped they wouldn't be disappointed at not finding toys inside.

But she needn't have worried. When the little girls unveiled their brightly colored jumpers with flowered, lace-collared shirts for underneath, matching tights, Mary Jane shoes, and the headbands and beaded necklaces and bracelets she'd topped it all off with for fun, they were every bit as thrilled as if they'd discovered a whole treasure trove of toys.

"Wow," Cully said as his daughters sorted through everything, each comparing with the other to see if they both had the same things.

"When I told the saleswoman at the store that I was thinking about buying the dresses for Amy and Randa

Culhane but didn't know their sizes she said the store keeps track of that on a card.''

"That's because I'm usually stoppin' in there without the girls and without checkin' on what size I got for them the time before, so the folks over there took pity on me and started to keep a record.''

And then there was the issue of the clothes being dresses. For the second time in just a short while her father came to Ivey's mind. "I know you must not be crazy about the idea of putting them in dresses, but—''

"It isn't that I care about the girls wearin' them. I just don't have the foggiest idea how to turn out little females. Plus, the few dresses they had when their mother left were ruined in the washing machine. Around our place we do all right with laundry that's full of jeans and overalls and plain old shirts and socks, but stick in that lacy stuff or those hose kind of stockings, and they come out lookin' worse than they go in.''

"Is that why you don't put the girls in dresses?'' Ivey asked.

"That's why.''

She couldn't help laughing at that, feeling a sudden welcome relief to learn he had such a practical reason that wasn't at all like her father's desire to reshape her and Savannah into the boys he'd rather have had.

Luckily—and purely coincidentally—the clothes were all made of easy-care fabrics, which Ivey explained to him, adding a few instructions about hand washing the tights.

"These are pretty big gifts,'' he said then, clearly curious as to why she'd gone to such an extreme.

She couldn't tell him that some of what had spurred her had to do with testing him to see how he'd respond, even though she hadn't realized that was a motive until just now, when he'd passed with flying colors. So instead she told him the other reason.

"I just couldn't resist dressing them up. I kept thinking of Savannah and myself as kids and how much we would have loved having those clothes."

Cully seemed to accept that. "Well, looks like you called it right for these two, too."

By then Amy and Randa were clamoring to change into their new outfits.

"Let's wait until tomorrow," Cully said in answer to that. "You can wear them to the Harvest Festival. Get all dressed up."

The two tiny imps argued with him but finally settled on wearing the beaded necklaces and bracelets, and slipping the headbands on—which set their choppy hair sticking out around them like the Statue of Liberty's crown.

"Can Ivey go with us to the Harbest Festibal?" Randa said then, as if it would be a consolation for having to wait to wear her new clothes.

"Maybe if we ask real nice she'll do it so she can see how you guys will look," Cully said, answering his daughter, but looking at Ivey as he did.

"Can you?" Amy asked, sounding like it would be a treat for them.

But the real treat in it would be for Ivey. "I'd like that," she said to Cully, then included the girls by playfully plucking at a few sprigs of their sticking-up hair.

With that settled, she lured them all into the dining room for dinner.

Amy and Randa's constant chatter through the meal of fried chicken, mashed potatoes, gravy, creamed corn, salad and then chocolate cake for dessert helped

Ivey not dwell too much on what had happened with Arlen.

She wasn't sure the same was true of Cully.

He was unusually quiet and kept a close eye on her as the four of them ate. Not that he was rude about it, or stared overtly. But Ivey could feel his gaze drifting to her more often than not, studying her, as if he were watching for signs of any lingering effects.

And there were lingering effects, even when she tried to forget about the incident, but she wasn't sure how obvious they were. Her hands were slightly shaky. Sometimes when she laughed at what one of the kids said it was a bit more loudly than was called for. And she didn't have any appetite at all. But she tried hard to be a bright, cheery and lighthearted hostess just the same.

When they'd finished the meal Cully checked the time. "There's a movie the girls might like on television about now. Mind if they watch it?" he asked.

She didn't and told him so, insisting that he stay at the table while she showed his daughters upstairs where she had the portable TV on the dresser in her room.

But when she got back downstairs Cully wasn't still sitting at the table. In fact, he had half of it cleared and was gathering more dishes to take into the kitchen.

"Hey, I didn't invite you here to clean up," she said as she rejoined him.

He didn't respond to that. "Are the girls all set?" he asked instead.

"I have them lying on Savannah's old bed. They snuggled right in."

"They'll probably fall asleep watching their movie."

Between the two of them Cully and Ivey took what was left on the dining room table into the kitchen where Ivey scraped the food into a plastic trash bag because there wasn't a garbage disposal.

"How about coffee or brandy?" she asked as she did.

"How about we wash the dishes instead?"

She thought about protesting against making a guest do that, but somehow she felt a need to put things in order and so rinsed the dishes and then filled the sink with soapy water rather than pursuing it.

Cully leaned his jean-clad hips against the edge of the counter beside her at the sink, towel at the ready to dry.

"So," he said.

"So," she repeated, knowing what was coming—the subject that had been hanging in the air between them all through dinner, just waiting to be addressed once Amy and Randa weren't there to overhear.

"So that's the guy you were going to marry," Cully said.

Just the thought of it sent a fresh shiver up Ivey's spine. "Arlen Earl Brunswell," she confirmed.

"What was he doing here? Besides lookin' to hurt you?"

"He wanted his engagement ring back. Understandably. It was an expensive piece of jewelry."

"Did you give it to him?"

"Sure. Right away. I had it in the desk. I've been thinking all week about the best way to return it. Somehow what went on tonight wasn't one of the ways I'd considered," she said, feebly trying to make light of it.

It didn't work. Cully still watched her with a troubled expression darkening his ice blue eyes as he dried the dishes she handed him.

"Did he always treat you like that?" he asked then.

"Yes and no. The name-calling and put-down stuff started after we got engaged, so yes, he had done that before. It was a contributing factor in my not going through with the wedding. I was thinking about that till-death-do-we-part stuff and how it would mean listening to his snide comments for the rest of my life. But no, I've never seen him as mad or as..."

"Violent?" Cully supplied the word when she stalled over it.

Somehow that seemed too strong a term. Maybe because in spite of how afraid she'd been of Arlen tonight, in spite of his hurting her arm and seeming as if he could have done a lot worse, she still felt somehow responsible, guilty, as if she'd driven him to behave that way, even though she knew that nothing—not even her leaving him at the altar—made his actions acceptable.

"He was over the edge tonight," she agreed, softening the description of it.

"Over the edge," Cully repeated. "There's no excuse for it, you know."

"I know. At least a part of me does."

"Is there another part that doesn't?"

"The part that feels bad about running out on the wedding. About embarrassing him so badly."

"Seems to me running out on a wedding that would have tied you to a person like that was the best thing you could have done."

"You mean that being commitment-shy saved me from a miserable marriage?" She attempted another joke. "No, the best thing I could have done was to have had better judgment of the kind of person he was in the first place and never gotten as far as the wedding at all.''

Cully inclined his head and raised an eyebrow, apparently agreeing with that without actually saying anything. ''I hate to think what it would have been like if you were married to him.''

She'd been thinking the same thing off and on all evening. Wondering if the humiliation of being left at the altar had provoked a response that nothing else ever would have. Or if what she'd seen in Arlen tonight was what she'd thought it was at the time—yet another level to him that would have been reached sooner or later. A very big flaw in his character that she'd overlooked.

She thought it was most likely another personality and character flaw that she'd overlooked. And it was unnerving to be faced with even more evidence of what a poor judge of the man she'd been.

But she didn't want to talk about that with Cully. She just wanted to concentrate on seeing him more clearly than she'd seen Arlen. If she was capable of it.

''I didn't thank you for coming to my rescue,'' she said instead of responding to his comment about what it might have been like to have gone through with marrying Arlen. She wasn't sure whether that thought or the memory of what had actually happened caused her voice to sound unsteady, but that's how it came out, telling her she was still shook-up by the turn things had taken.

''Arlen Earl Brunswell should be the one thankin' me.''

''For what?''

''For not givin' him the beating of his life.''

"Did it scare Amy and Randa to see what was going on when you guys drove up?"

"They didn't have much of an idea about what was happening, so no, it didn't seem to. And you heard what was on their minds after the fact. They were wound up but not scared. I think to be scared they'd have had to feel threatened themselves and there was no reason for them to feel that way. I had them locked safe and sound in the truck before I came in the house."

"I'm glad. What an awful thing for them to come in on."

"What a lousy thing for *you* to be in on."

"I'm just glad it didn't get any worse than it did. And that it's over."

"Is it?"

The question seemed very pointed. "Do you mean is the relationship over? Absolutely no doubt about it."

"But is he going to show up here again?"

That thought sent another shudder through her. "He doesn't have any reason to. I don't have anything else that belongs to him," she said. "And even if he does, I won't let him in again, that's for sure."

"And you'll call me the minute it happens, if it does."

It wasn't a question. It was an order. But one that made her feel better to know she had Cully close by if she needed him.

She smiled up at him, albeit wanly. "I may not know Arlen as well as I thought, but I can just about guarantee that he won't risk running into you again by coming to Elk Creek."

"But if he shows up here you'll call me," Cully reiterated.

"But if he shows up here I'll call you," she agreed.

They'd finished the dishes by then and Ivey offered him coffee or an after dinner drink again.

"Pour us each another glass of wine while I go up and check on the girls," he suggested.

She took the wine and two clean glasses into the living room but not without checking the back door to make sure it was locked good and tight.

In the living room she set the wine and glasses on a round table that still held her father's checkerboard and pulled the drapes closed over the picture window before returning to pour the wine. As she did she couldn't help thinking about her father, about Arlen.

As harsh a father as Silas had been, he hadn't been a hitter. Only once had he raised a hand to Savannah, but other than that his unpleasantness and reprimands had all been verbal, his punishments in the form of more and harder work that nearly broke their backs but that never involved physical violence.

But things were different with Arlen. He'd hurt her tonight. Gone on hurting her even after she'd told him his grip on her arm was causing her pain. And she didn't doubt that had Cully not come in when he did, her former fiancé would have taken it further. That he would have made her get on her knees to him. That he could well have struck her.

She'd grown up convinced that she could spot from a mile away any man as unkind as her father. And that once she'd spotted him, she could avoid ever having such a person in her life. But now she realized that Arlen had been even worse.

And yet when she'd met him she'd thought he was exactly the opposite of anything her father was.

How could she have been so wrong?

And what if she *had* married him?

That thought made her shudder all over again and seemed like glaring proof that she really couldn't trust her judgment.

Cully came back downstairs just then and she told herself she should ask him to leave. She should put distance between them and keep it there because not getting involved was the only way she could be sure she wasn't headed for more mistakes.

But she couldn't make herself do it.

As much as she told herself not to trust her own opinion of any man, to be wary of her feelings, Cully's being there gave her a sense of security, as if he were a safe harbor from a rough storm at sea.

"How are the girls?" she asked when she turned and brought the wineglasses with her to sit on the couch.

Cully sat next to her. "They're sound asleep. But they got into some trouble up there."

Ivey handed him his glass but without even taking a sip of it, he set it on the coffee table and angled his big body so he was sitting sideways on the sofa, facing her. Then he took her by the arms and angled her the same way in front of him, with her back to him so he could knead the spot on either side of her neck where it curved into her shoulders.

She didn't know how he knew her muscles were in knots there, but his strong hands applying just the right amount of pressure in a slow, firm massage began to break them up.

Ivey set her glass on the table, too, so she could just give herself over to his ministrations. "What did they do?" she asked, referring to Amy and Randa.

"Uh..." He chuckled slightly. "I'm afraid they got

into your drawers and helped themselves to some pretty racy nightclothes.''

Ivey laughed, too, even as she felt a blush rise in her cheeks. ''The first suitcase I brought here was packed with things for my honeymoon.'' Including two sheer nighties—one black lace and the other white silk that left very little to the imagination.

''No wonder that guy was so mad. If I'd missed out on those I'd be pretty het up myself,'' Cully teased.

''Arlen didn't know what was in store for him.''

''Good thing or he'd have been in worse shape tonight.'' Cully bent close enough to her ear for her to feel the warmth of his breath against her skin. ''My girls don't do them justice, though,'' he added with another chuckle, this one with a sensuous rumble to it.

While his right hand went on massaging the lee of her neck he reached his left arm around the front of her to her right shoulder and pulled her to rest against him.

It was strange how powerful was the effect of suddenly being in the circle of his arm, braced by his big body. For the first time since Arlen had arrived on her doorstep, Ivey felt every ounce of tension drain away as if the plug had been pulled on it.

She tilted her chin high and to the side so she could look back at him, at that supple mouth with its oh-so-sexy lips. ''It's okay that Amy and Randa played dress-up. I don't mind,'' she said but her voice came out softly, sounding as relaxed as she felt.

Cully just nodded, distractedly, as if his daughters' mischief wasn't foremost on his mind.

Then he bent his head low enough to press those lips to hers as his left hand rose to her jawbone, to the spot behind her ear, his fingertips alone running from there in featherlight strokes down the corded and very sensitive tendon stretched taut by the backward angle of her head.

At first Ivey just let him kiss her. Slow, sweet, gentle kisses that she barely returned. Kisses that were pure enticement, beckoning her to shed all the ugliness of what had happened earlier, to forget it, to indulge herself in this that was a much, much better use of her thoughts, her emotions.

And how could she not indulge herself when it felt so good? When being wrapped in his arms calmed her every fear, renewed her, made her feel whole again…

She began to answer his kisses with some of her own. To part her lips when he parted his. To meet his tongue when it came calling. To dance and parry with it and even chase it into his mouth to do some exploring herself as the tension he'd drained out of her was replaced by something more than the pure relaxation that had suffused her before.

Passion, desire, sprang to life, initially in tiny embers that grew lazily into flames.

Cully's hand trailed from her collarbone, slipping just inside the V of her sweater. But not nearly as far inside of it as she discovered she wanted him to go. Her breasts craved his touch; her nipples tightened like tiny rosebuds awaiting his caress to allow them to blossom.

She turned slightly more toward him, hoping that might relay the message that she wanted, needed, so much more of him, of his hands on her.

As if he were in tune enough to know, he traced a path lower still, brushing across the taut crest of her breast without stopping to actually grasp it the way she wished he would. Teasing her with those featherlight fingertips that traveled round and round it, barely touching her at all yet driving her even wilder with wanting him, until her nipple was pinched so tight it almost hurt.

Only then did he close his whole hand over it, easing some of that yearning in the firm caress of his palm.

Very slowly he began to knead her breast, gently squeezing, releasing, squeezing again, rubbing just enough to torment her anew.

It all felt so good she could hardly bear it. Her head fell back to his shoulder as a sigh of pleasure escaped her lips, as her body responded to him with a will of its own, as desire sweet and warm rolled through her whole body.

She wanted him to take her upstairs. To make love to her. She wanted to bask in his touch all the night through, to fall asleep in his arms....

But then she remembered that his daughters were upstairs.

And with that memory came others. Of the earlier events of the evening.

Of her own fear that she couldn't trust her judgment of men, her judgment even of Cully...

"I think we better stop," she said in a weak, breathy whisper.

But it was enough for Cully to do just that, to slide his wonderful, seeking hand away from her breast, back up to her neck.

For a long moment he just held her that way. She could actually feel his heart pounding against her back, and the hard ridge of his desire for her pressing against her hip let her know just how much he wanted her, how much of an effort it was taking to end prematurely what they'd begun.

When he finally had control again he said, "I shouldn't have done this. I'm sorry."

"No, no, don't apologize," she answered. "This was good...too good... It's just that—"

"Tonight was not the right night for it," he finished for her.

He took a deep, ragged breath, sighed it out and she saw him glance at the ceiling as if he could see his daughters through it. "Tonight was definitely not the right time." Another sigh, this one reluctant but resigned. "I should get those girls home."

Ivey sat up—not wanting to leave his embrace but knowing if she stayed against him she wasn't going to have the will to break away at all.

"Why don't you just let them spend the night?" she suggested. "They're already asleep and since we're all going to the Harvest Festival tomorrow I could help them into their new dresses and you could pick us all up. How would that be?"

Cully's handsome face eased into a lazy, lopsided grin. "You're goin' to let my kids spend the night and send me home?" he joked.

"Sorry," Ivey answered with a smile of her own at the irony of it when she would much rather he be the one staying, too.

"Well, I guess that would work out," he finally conceded. "But it's a terrible thing to make a man jealous of his own kids."

The passion that had ignited between them was only hiding behind their teasing, but still it helped that he was making light of this.

Once more Ivey joked, "I can't have you staying, too. I just don't have any more nightgowns." She'd meant for him to wear but that wasn't how it had come out.

Cully's expression turned downright devilish. "Perfect."

He pushed himself off the couch, headed for the entryway, and for a minute Ivey thought he was calling her bluff and heading upstairs.

But then he took a sharp left turn and went to the front door.

She joined him there, welcomed by the warmth of his pale blue eyes watching her as she did.

"About eleven or so tomorrow?" he asked.

"Whatever you say."

"And if you hear so much as a bump in the night you'll call me?"

"Especially with Amy and Randa here," she assured.

Cully's gaze searched her face, his own features sobering. "Are you sure you're okay?"

As far as the tension Arlen had caused, she really was okay again. But as far as the sexual tension Cully had just raised in her? That was definitely not so okay. It was still raging inside her, trying to make her start up what she'd just cut short.

But she couldn't give in. And she couldn't let Cully know how much her body was crying out for her to. So instead she said, "I'm fine. Thanks to you."

He saluted her with two fingers to an imaginary hat brim. "The cavalry to the rescue," he joked.

Then he bent toward her for another very tempting kiss, lingering to the brink of taking her in his arms again before he ended it.

"Lock up after me," he ordered.

"I will."

He cast her one last glance and then left. She knew he was waiting just outside to hear the lock click and only after it did, did his boot heels make their hollow thuds on her porch, down her steps to the silence of the soil below as he went to his truck.

Ivey waited in the entrance until she heard him drive off, all the while wishing he really was her overnight guest.

But it was better that he wasn't, she told herself. Better that she'd slowed things down, given herself more time.

It was just hard to believe when the memory of how good it had felt to be in his arms, to have his hands on her, followed her all the way up to bed.

Chapter Eight

"Jus' wait'll Daddy sees us!" Amy gushed when she and Randa were dressed the next morning.

Ivey had helped them into their new outfits and French braided their hair—using the headbands to hold back the shortest lengths on top and at the sides. The two of them looked adorable as they turned this way and that standing on a chair in front of the mirror above the sink in the bathroom.

Ivey had showered and washed her own hair early, letting it air-dry and scrunching her curls into place every few minutes along the way. The little girls were enthralled with the process, just as they were by watching her apply her light, freckle-hiding makeup, cheekbone-enhancing blush and eye-darkening mascara.

They were also interested in watching her put on the lightweight hunter green sweater dress she chose to wear, with its high banded collar, deep-cut sleeveless armholes that left her shoulders exposed, and buttons from the neck down the straight uninterrupted line to the hem that reached her dress boots.

With the three of them ready to go, Ivey folded the clothes and shoes the kids had had on the night before and put them into a grocery sack.

"Okay, we're all set. Let's go down and wait for your dad," she told them, leading the way and taking with her the sack and a blazer that matched her dress and would serve to cover her bare arms for the after-dark chill.

"When will Daddy be here?" Amy asked anxiously as they neared the entryway.

"Anytime now," Ivey answered, feeling every bit as eager for Cully to arrive.

"Will he know we're us?" This from Randa who gave a very unladylike tug to her tights.

"You mean because you're so dressed up?"

"I don't think we never looked like this before," the tiny imp confirmed.

Ivey laughed. "Oh, I think he'll still know you."

Cully's truck pulled up out front just then and before Ivey could stop them, Amy and Randa threw open the front door and charged onto the porch.

"Lookit us! Lookit us!" Amy called to him.

Ivey set her blazer and the sack of the kids' clothes beside the door and went outside, too, so she could see for herself Cully's reaction to his daughters.

He rounded the truck and came to a stop at the foot of the steps. Tipping his Stetson farther back on his head with a single thumb to the brim, he stared at the two girls where they stood for his inspection on the porch's edge.

"Would you look at this? Are these two gorgeous

little girls my Amy and Randa? Ooo-ee! I can hardly believe what I'm seein', you're both so pretty!''

They giggled with delight and jumped off the porch into his arms like the two ragamuffins they still were underneath.

Cully caught them, put one on each of his hips as if they were no bigger than babies and kissed them in turn.

Then he carried them up the steps, focusing on Ivey as he walked to within a few feet of her. ''And who do we have here? Another blindin' beauty, that's for sure,'' he said, his ice blue eyes running the length of her from curly head to toe and back again. His lips stretched into a lazy, appreciative grin that had a much more seductive hint to it than the one he'd bestowed on his daughters.

''Tha's Ivey,'' Randa supplied as if he'd lost his mind. Then, across his chest the youngest Culhane said to her sister, ''He knew'd we were us, but he didn't know'd Ivey was her.''

''I think he's funnin',''Amy answered.

Ivey could have kissed him for his response to his daughters because a small part of her had still fretted that he might react the way her own father would have to her and Savannah being decked out in girlish finery. But then, she could have kissed him just for the heck of it, too.

He was dressed in what she guessed he'd probably consider his good blue jeans, with a white shirt tucked into them and a braided leather string tie hanging loosely from under the open collar.

His lean, tanned face was clean shaven, and he smelled of that cool mountain night aftershave. It occurred to Ivey, as the warmth of his gaze washed over her and sent a thrill all through her with nothing more than that, that her feelings for him were deepening at a rapid rate she couldn't control even when she tried.

He leaned forward, pretending to take a closer look at her. "Why, I'll be darned. It is Ivey. I guess I must be the luckiest man in this whole town for gettin' to take the three most beautiful women to this festival today."

Amy and Randa giggled again.

"The luckiest and most full-of-bull man in this whole town," Ivey teased, enjoying the flattery anyway.

He let Amy and Randa slide down his sides to stand on their own and pecked a quick kiss on Ivey's mouth, surprising her.

"Hi, there," he said in a cozy tone that was clearly for her alone.

"Morning."

"Things go all right here through the night?"

"Just fine. The girls and I have been up since the crack of dawn, having a great time together."

"Ivey maked'd us special toast with syrup on it like pancakes," Randa offered by way of confirmation.

"And she fixed our hair so it doesn't look like we got caught in the thresher," Amy added.

"I can see that," Cully said without taking his eyes off Ivey.

"Can we go now?" Randa asked.

"Are we all set to?" he asked Ivey.

"I just need to grab my jacket and the girls' things from inside and close the door. Why don't you get them in the truck while I do?"

"Sure you don't need my help?" he asked with hopeful insinuation.

"I think I can manage," Ivey answered wryly.

"Too bad," he said in a near whisper before he herded his daughters to the truck and followed them to lift them into the cab.

Ivey could tell Cully was full of the devil today. It was there in the cocky quirk of his mouth, the tone of his voice, the glimmer in his eye, even in the slightly more exaggerated swagger of his terrific hips. There was an air about him that said he was feeling carefree, high-spirited, rarin' to go and ready to have a good time.

It was infectious. And it was also a nice change from Arlen's intensity and stuffiness, or the grumbling she would have met from her father even just asking to attend an occasion like this.

But Arlen and her father were the last people she wanted to think about today, so Ivey did what she'd said she was going to—she reached inside the door for the grocery sack and her jacket, locked and shut it once she had, and followed the threesome to the truck.

The Harvest Festival—like all of Elk Creek's cele-brations—was held in and around the park square. Cully stopped a block before that and pulled into the school parking lot that was already nearly full. They met up with his brothers there, as well as Jackson, his wife and stepdaughter, Meggie.

The town was so small that it was a lot like one big family anyway, so it seemed perfectly natural to mingle the Culhane clan with the Hellers as they all walked that last block. In front of the courthouse they met up with Beth's small family; Linc, Kansas and Danny; and even Della and Bucky Dennehy and their brood, adding to their ranks.

Since October's weather could be unreliable it had

become a matter of course to erect yellow-and-white striped tents for this particular celebration, all of them positioned around the gazebo in the center of the park.

But with the temperatures headed for the low seventies the sides of all the tents were drawn up, displaying the picnic tables arranged under the one where hot dogs, hamburgers and sausage sandwiches were already being cooked and sold for lunch. Two other tents shaded games of chance, and a fourth had folding tables laden with pies, cakes, cookies, muffins and a whole variety of home-canned goods from area harvests that judges sampled and awarded ribbons and prizes for.

At various spots outside the tents other competitions were about to begin, among them mutton busting for four-, five- and six-year-old kids.

"We better get you signed up," Yance said to Amy when the last call for it went out over the loudspeaker.

Both Yance and Clint had fussed over Amy's and Randa's new clothes, using some of that irresistible Culhane charm on the two tiny girls and clearly thrilling them. But now Clint shook his head fatalistically and said, "She can't be hangin' on to the back of a racin' sheep in a dress."

"It'd wreck it," Amy agreed.

"We can go back to the truck and put on your overalls from last night," Cully suggested to his daughter. "Or you can just skip it."

Ivey saw Amy's dilemma in the child's expression as Amy tried to decide on a course of action. She thought she understood it. In Amy's place Ivey would have given up the dress to please her father and prove she could hold her own with the boys he admired. But she wouldn't have wanted to.

She was all set to step in on Amy's behalf against the three indomitable Culhanes when Amy said an easy, "Okay." And then turned to Ivey. "But if my hair gets messed up will you fix it?"

It was on the tip of Ivey's tongue to tell the little girl she didn't have to do this if she didn't want to. But as she studied Amy she didn't see any signs that pointed to anything but the child being anxious to compete. So instead she merely said, "Sure."

Then she watched Amy slip her hand into her father's and excitedly skip along beside him back to the school parking lot.

It was that sight that made Ivey realize there was a difference in the child's attitude about this than what she would have felt herself in similar circumstances. There was none of the resentment she would have suffered. Amy was as enthusiastic about competing as her father and her uncles were on her behalf. And it didn't have anything to do with making her more like a boy. It was purely for the fun of it.

It occurred to Ivey then that maybe she ought to loosen up. That she was making a bigger deal out of things in her mind than they were for anyone actually involved in them. That she was bringing too much of her own baggage into this and that it was about time she let it go and relaxed.

Chill out and quit comparing Amy and Randa to you and Savannah, she told herself firmly.

It wasn't difficult to embrace the advice because it was so freeing, allowing Ivey to join wholeheartedly in cheering Amy on by the time the contest was ready to begin. In fact, she let herself get so caught up in the comical event that she shouted encouragement with the rest of the crowd.

And it was comical.

Intended to mimic rodeo bronco busting, each child in turn strapped a bicycle helmet on their head, climbed onto the back of a sheep that was being held steady, clamped their legs around the animal's sides and leaned forward so they could wrap their arms around the neck as if they were giving the animal a big hug. Then the sheep was let loose.

Hanging on was the goal—for a full six seconds during which judges awarded points for form. But as far as Ivey could see, form was at a minimum and for most kids doing well meant just keeping from losing their grip and sliding off before the buzzer sounded.

It was like watching slapstick. Some kids lost the grip of their legs but still managed to cling to the sheep's neck, running alongside and trying to hop back on before giving up the ghost. Some seemed left hanging in midair as the sheep dashed forward out from under them before they realized the animal had been released. While others dived off as if the sheep were a springboard into a pool.

Even the ones who finished the ride were funny to watch as they did everything they could think of to keep their seat through the quick jostle.

No one got hurt, even the kids who fell off took it in stride, and no matter what, each child received a huge round of applause, hoots and hollers, and an ice-cream bar for their effort.

Amy's French braid ended up a bare glimmer of its former self but she won a blue ribbon for the four-year-old category and rejoined their group with a proud grin that resembled the one Cully beamed her way.

Cully, Clint and Yance treated her like a gold medal Olympic winner and the little girl basked in her glory for a while before demanding that her dress clothes be put back on and her hair be recombed.

Cully didn't balk. "So what do you say?" he asked Ivey once he'd agreed to take Amy back to the truck. "Will you come along as hairdresser to the star?"

"Absolutely."

"Good, because I think we need some female assistance with those hose things—"

"Tights," Amy corrected as if she'd done it before.

"Tights," Cully amended. "It's one thing to take 'em off but I can't say I've ever put any on," he said, tossing Ivey a wicked smile.

Ivey laughed, borrowed a comb from Della, and she, Cully and Amy headed for the school parking lot.

As Amy walked slightly ahead of them, strutting her stuff and making them laugh at her, Cully reached an arm around Ivey's shoulders to pull her close to his side. "I'm glad you're here with us today," he said in a voice for her ears alone.

"Me, too," she admitted, feeling a rush of electricity all through her at his touch, at the sound of his voice, the feel of his big body against hers, the warmth of his breath on her skin.

Oh, yeah, she was definitely glad to be there with him!

And she definitely had feelings for him. *Deep* feelings for him that made her pulse race at being so near to him. That gave her a sort of rosy blush from the inside out. That gave her the sense of being complete only when she was with him.

She really was on thin ice with this man.

But suddenly she just didn't care about proceeding with caution.

Being with him felt too good. *She* felt too good. Too good to worry about it anymore.

Today was a day of celebration. Of fun. Of forgetting the past and escaping cares. At least for a while. And she set her mind to doing just that.

With Amy looking like a little china doll again they caught up with everybody back in the lunch tent for some of the hamburgers and hot dogs. Then they all took on the afternoon with gusto.

The Culhanes, Linc, Jackson, and their brother-in-law Ash Blackwolf played as hard as they worked, and when Ivey wasn't off with Beth, Ally, Kansas, Della and the kids, she was watching the men compete in the log-throwing contest, calf roping, bull riding and barrel racing.

By the end of the day the men were all full of dirt, dust and grime and while the women put together the potluck supper in the churchyard they all loaded into trucks and disappeared for an hour to clean up.

Ivey missed Cully while he was gone but it was worth the wait. He came back with his face shaved clean of the day's growth of beard and his hair freshly washed. He was dressed in black cowboy boots; tight, tight black jeans; and a silver-gray western shirt with a red-and-pink arrowhead design above each of two breast pockets. He looked so handsome that one glance at him, at the smile of pleasure that erupted on his face when his eyes met hers, set off a ripple of delight in her.

She'd had a great time with him and with everybody else throughout the day, but just then what she wanted more than anything was to be alone with him. To slip away into the darkness that was falling beyond the lantern lights strung from the church out to the trees that surrounded it and have Cully all to herself.

And as hard as she tried to curb that desire because she knew it couldn't be, it stayed with her like an itch she couldn't scratch.

Supper was a sampling of the best dishes the best cooks in town could come up with but Ivey's only appetite was for Cully and she hardly touched even the small amount of food she took.

All the while her mind wandered to ways she might be able to get him alone. She actually considered pretending she didn't feel well or had twisted her ankle and needed to go home. Or maybe she could spill something down the front of her that might require a change of clothes back at her house. While he waited downstairs. And maybe he would need to zip up what she changed into…something slinky…

She was getting carried away, she told herself with a yank of her thoughts back into reality. Maybe she'd loosened up *too* much.

When supper was finally over everyone walked across to where a local band had set up in the gazebo to play music for dancing. At least if she couldn't be alone with Cully she could be in his arms, she thought.

But even that proved frustrating because with the shortage of women in the small town there were so many partners vying for dances that she couldn't refuse them.

Cully reluctantly relinquished her to his friends and brothers for several turns around the dance floor, but each time it was still Cully she would rather have been with, Cully who was on her mind the whole time. Cully's arms she wanted around her. Cully's teasing she wanted to have whispered in her ear.

As temperatures cooled the crowd thinned out and before it was too late Yance and Clint offered to take a weary Amy and Randa home. Ivey liked the other two Culhane brothers but that offer increased her fondness for them a hundredfold because it meant that at least she and Cully would be by themselves for the drive back to her place.

Cully said good-night to his daughters and then asked Ivey to dance again. But over her shoulder he seemed to be watching to make sure his family was out of sight before he said, "The trouble with stayin' here is that I have to share you. Look at all those guys on the sidelines just waitin' to cut in."

"We don't have to stay," she said, sounding a lot more innocent than she felt.

Cully reared back just enough to look down at her, clearly only pretending to be surprised that his leading statement had produced the results he'd apparently had in mind. "You wouldn't mind leavin'?"

"There's still the rest of the bottle of wine from last night. We could go home where it's quiet, have a glass..." She couldn't believe her own boldness. But there was something about the day that had left her feeling uninhibited, inclined to follow her instincts. And at that moment her instincts were all urging her to get herself at least a small part of this day alone with Cully. No matter what it took.

"Wine and quiet sound good," he agreed.

And that was all there was to it. Holding hands, they made the rounds saying good-night and then headed for the school parking lot and Cully's truck.

Ivey laughed suddenly as he helped her into the driver's side to sit in the middle of the bench seat rather than remove the sack that held Amy and Randa's clothes on the passenger's side. "Why do I feel like a teenager sneaking away from a football game I'm supposed to sit through to the end?"

"Same principle," he answered with an ornery half smile. "Slippin' off to be by ourselves..." he let his voice trail off suggestively.

"Something you did a lot of?" she teased.

"My fair share."

"So you know all the ins and outs."

"Want me to teach 'em to you, teach?" he offered, his voice full of lasciviousness as he turned the truck onto the road home.

"Is there more to it than we've just done?"

"Teenagers wouldn't have said good-night and announced what they were doin'. Sets tongues to waggin'."

"And ruins reputations," she played along.

"So I guess by sayin' good-night and makin' it look like everything's innocent, we've covered our tracks," he said, casting her a sideways glance.

"Isn't it innocent?"

He just smiled at her without answering.

"But you don't think we set any tongues to wagging?" she said.

"Do you care if we did?"

He made it sound so wickedly delicious and daring that Ivey laughed again as he turned onto the drive that led to her house. "Think the gossip would follow me all the way back to my kindergarten class in Cheyenne?"

"Might. Want to risk it?"

They were only joking but it occurred to Ivey that right then she would risk just about anything to be with him. "Too late. I think I already have."

''Does that mean I get to come in after all?''

''What kind of a hostess would I be if I invited you over for a glass of wine and then reneged?''

Cully parked in front of the porch and stopped the engine. He angled himself on the seat in her direction, stretching a long arm across the back, reaching around and fingering a few curls on the right side of her head. ''What if I said I didn't give a damn about havin' a glass of wine? That I really just wanted to get you alone?'' His voice was soft, seductive, and it sent hot lava through her veins.

''What if I said I didn't care about the wine, either, and I'd just wanted to get *you* alone?'' she heard herself answer before she'd considered it, her own voice as full of intimacy as his was.

His mouth stretched into a wide grin even as his thick brows dipped into a fleeting frown. ''I'd say great minds work alike and I'm glad of it. But I'm also afraid you might not be sure about this.''

Was she sure? Was she sure that she wanted him to take her inside, upstairs, to kiss her, to hold her, to touch her? That she didn't want tonight to end, not now, not after a glass of wine, not after a few kisses on the couch, not until daybreak? Maybe not even then?

''I think I'm sure,'' she whispered, trying not to nuzzle against his hand where it toyed with her hair.

He chuckled. ''Is thinkin' you're sure the same as bein' sure?''

''Close enough,'' she said, hoping he couldn't hear the pounding of her heart but thinking that he might be able to since it was so loud in her own ears.

His eyes captured hers in the dim glow cast inside

the truck cab by her porch light, searching them as if
to see into her mind.

He must have found what he was looking for because he bent forward enough to kiss her. One of those
slow, soft, chaste kisses, almost as if he were testing
the waters.

Then he pulled back, opened the door and got down,
holding his hand out to her to join him.

Ivey was operating on automatic pilot by then, not
thinking about anything but the way this man made her
feel, wanting him, needing him, indulging herself for
once....

She slipped her hand into his much bigger, leathery
one and slid out of the truck, too.

They held hands all the way up the porch steps
where she took her key out of one of her jacket pockets
and unlocked the front door. Then she led the way
inside, still holding Cully's hand to bring him with her.

He closed and locked the door behind them but neither of them turned on a light. Instead, with his back
to the door he drew her closer and kissed her again,
this time not so slowly, not so softly, not so chastely,
but playfully nonetheless.

His lips parted over hers, his tongue teased hers
open, flicking against her teeth, testing the edges, dart-
ing inside only to dance back out again the moment
she met it with her own.

He didn't stop kissing her but he began to ease her
toward the stairs, stopping at the bottom of them to
take off her blazer and drape it over the newel post.
Then his hands came to her bare shoulders, cupping
them, giving a gentle massage that chased away any
lingering tension, that left her feeling pliable beneath
the mastery of his touch and just a scant bit aroused....

But aroused enough to take one of those hands away a few moments later, using it to lead him up the steps, stopping at the top to kiss him this time.

Regardless of who instigated it, their kisses were growing deeper, more hungry with every passing moment as playfulness turned to passion.

Cully took the initiative this time and urged her to the nearest bedroom—her room—where he brought them to a stop at the foot of her bed.

His hands were on her shoulders again, kneading them the way he'd kneaded her breasts the night before, reminding her of how wonderful it had felt, building within her a need to feel it again.

He gently pushed her to sit on the bed, abandoning her mouth and bending over her to pick up one of her feet. She felt like Cinderella in reverse since her glass slippers were coming off instead of going on. But she didn't doubt for a moment that Cully was her Prince Charming as he placed a kiss on each of her knees just before removing her boots in turn.

Then he pulled her to stand before him again, covering her mouth with his once more as he began to unfasten the buttons of her dress.

They were of a like mind in that, as well. And since he'd started it, she didn't feel too shy about doing her part. She reached to the collar of his shirt, popping open the snaps that held it closed, pulling it free of his jeans when she neared the waistband so she could finish the job.

She slid her hands inside of it, to the warm, smooth skin of his chest, to hard pectorals and broad shoulders, unable to resist slipping the shirt off along the way, letting it fall to the floor around them.

He had her dress completely unbuttoned by then,

hanging loosely around her. She felt the cooler air of the room in the strip of bare skin exposed between her braless breasts, down her stomach to the bikini panties she had on. He spread the dress farther, unveiling her as if she were something very precious before he let the dress drop to keep his shirt company.

She thought he'd take her breasts in his hands then but he didn't. Instead he wrapped her in the circle of his strong arms, holding her, kissing her still, cherishing her.

She laid her flattened palms to the wide expanse of his back, reveling in the feel of the muscles beneath them, learning the texture of his skin where it sheathed those work-honed mounds of power.

Holding her firmly, he eased her back down onto the bed again, this time laying her there, joining her while he explored her mouth with his tongue, thrusting in and out like a sneak preview of things to come.

But still he didn't really touch her. He just went on holding her, until she thought she might go crazy with wanting so much more from him.

Then all at once he was gone.

He stood at the foot of the bed and made quick work of shedding his own boots, socks and jeans. If he'd had on underwear she didn't see any sign of it, but what she did see suddenly was Cully standing before her, completely naked and gloriously masculine.

It was a sight that took her breath away and even as much as she enjoyed it, it only doubled her desire for him, leaving her almost desperate to feel that incredible body against her own.

Still she was left wanting as he knelt on the bed beside her, bending over her to kiss her again, meeting her with only his mouth over hers as he reached for her panties and rolled them off.

Yes! Oh, yes! she thought. Now that they were both naked she was sure he would come to her, press himself to her, let her feel the whole length of him.

But instead, he stayed sitting on his haunches next to her, reaching for her only with his hands.

His fingertips alone stroked her skin like the soft hairs of a sable paintbrush. Along the sides of her face. The twin ridges of her jawbone. Down into the hollow of her throat. Spreading to the wings of her collarbone, to her shoulders, across the ultrasensitive insides of her arms...

Slow, sensuous brush strokes that barely touched her skin more than a silk slip might, but that lit a path of desire by ever so gently awakening her nerve endings, leaving them all alert, inflamed, yearning for so much more.

From her wrists his wondrous fingertips slid up again, a return trip to her shoulders, this time whispering across the sides of her breasts, just teasing on his way to her rib cage, to her stomach, to her hips.

Ivey couldn't help that her back arched in the wake of those hands, following the lure of his caress, craving the feel of it again.

But he was in no hurry.

He rose up on his knees so his hands could travel a tender trail down her legs, to her ankles, her feet, her toes, even as her eyes feasted on the sight of his broad chest and shoulders, on sculpted arms, on his flat stomach, on his big, powerful hands working their miracles on her skin.

Her knees fell slightly apart as if he'd relaxed her so completely that she didn't have the will to keep them closed, freeing the way for those fingertip strokes to retrace the path on the bare insides of her legs.

Oh, how she wanted him!

She reached out to him, thinking to inflict a little delicious torment of her own, laying her palms against his sides and smoothing her way upward and across, into the light smattering of hair where hardened male nibs nested.

It didn't take more urging than that for him to come back to her, to lie beside her, his hard, masculine body half covering her much curvier one.

He kissed her then. The spot behind her ear. Her lobe. The crest of her cheekbones, the tip of her nose, before covering her mouth with his, open, warm, only slightly moist, but urgent now.

His tongue charged in at hers, inviting it to play. Ivey accepted the invitation even as she lost some ground when his hand slipped over her breast the way she'd been craving and a sigh escaped her throat.

Gone were the light brush strokes of his fingertips, replaced by the firm grip of his kid leather hand. Kneading, squeezing, discovering the hardened peak where it strained in response to the delicate torture of fingers that sought it, circled it, rolled it as gently as if he were testing the texture of a pearl.

His mouth abandoned hers, kissing yet another path downward, leaving tiny, tantalizing tongue licks to air-dry.

One moment his hand was covering her nipple and the next his mouth was, surprising her even though it shouldn't have. Delighting her. Driving her passion, her desire, higher and higher.

Again the brush strokes of his fingertips trailed over her skin, this time slipping from the top of her thigh to the velvet inner flesh of it, to that spot that was already waiting for him, aching for him, wanting him.

One of Ivey's hands was in his hair, the other was on the iron solid bulge of his biceps, and it was that hand she put into motion herself, skipping across to his side, down to his hip, forward to the long, hard proof that he wanted her as much as she wanted him, that she could drive him as wild as he was driving her.

But Cully couldn't withstand all Ivey had.

He opened her thighs with an insistent knee of his own and found his place between them, probing, seeking, entering the warm, welcoming enclave of her body so smoothly, so completely, Ivey nearly cried out with the intense pleasure of it.

He kissed her again, a deep, openmouthed kiss, a mingling of his breath with hers, his tongue with hers, his whole body with hers, just before he began to move within her. First in just a pulsing. Then in a flex that sent him deeper into her, deeper still, before he drew partway out, only to plunge in again.

Ivey met him, matched him, thrust for thrust as long as she could keep up, feeling the storm building inside her, the mounting energy, the growing need.

Her hands were filled with the rolling muscles of his back; her senses were filled with the feel, the scent, the lingering taste of him. Her body was filled with his, and together they rode into the center of the storm where lightning struck them each at the same time. White-hot lightning, melding them together in an ecstasy so powerful Ivey was helpless to do anything but succumb to it, letting it carry her away on bolt after bolt of it, clinging to Cully as he drove them through the gale, exploding onto the other side of it....

Then slowly, bit by bit, the lightning ebbed, the storm calmed.

Cully came to rest with all his weight atop her, his breathing heavy and hot in her hair.

"I'm in love with you, Ivey," he confessed in a passion husky voice that sounded surprised at the revelation. Or maybe at the realization.

"I'm in love with you, too," she answered, knowing it for a fact only as the words came out.

But it was a fact. It was the heartfelt truth.

Cully kissed her eyes, Her nose. Her mouth. Then he left her, falling to his back and pulling her to lie on top of him now.

And that, too, felt incredibly good. Perfect. As if his body were the ideal cushion for hers.

He pulled the covers up over them both and then settled one arm around her, holding her, while his other hand cupped the back of her head and traced soft circles against her scalp. Circles that grew smaller, fainter, as he fell into a heavy slumber.

Ivey wasn't far behind. Her own breathing slowed, deepened. Her thoughts drifted, flowed dreamlike toward sleep, too.

And that was when she heard it.

Quietly.

As if from a distance.

Was she just imagining it...?

Or was she really hearing bells and whistles?

Chapter Nine

Even without Amy and Randa to pounce on him at dawn Cully woke up. In Ivey's bed. With Ivey in his arms. Sleeping peacefully, her soft breaths warm against his bare chest.

Lordy, but it felt good.

There was nowhere else in the world he'd rather be at that moment. No one else he'd rather be with.

He really was in love with Miss Ivey Heller. Head over heels, crazy in love. The kind of love, he realized, that made him want every morning for the rest of his life to be just this way—waking up in bed together, holding her, being able to open his eyes to her sweet face....

Knowing it didn't hit him like a bolt of lightning. Instead, as if the knowledge had been there forever and he'd just not recognized it before, it seeped into his conscious mind that he wanted her in his life for the long run.

That he wanted her as his wife.

He loved her. They were terrific together—in bed and out of it. She was terrific with his kids. Amy and Randa liked her. She'd be a great mother—to them and to a few more he'd like to have with her.

Funny, since Kim had walked out on him he'd wondered if he'd ever want to get married again. He'd doubted it. But here he was, after such a short time of getting reacquainted with Ivey, and he knew for a fact that that's just what he wanted—to get married again, to her.

He tightened his arms around her, feeling her small breasts against his side, wanting her, wanting to wake her, propose to her, then seal it by making love to her as the sun rose in the sky....

But into that plan flashed a memory that shot a hole through it.

Barely more than a week ago Ivey had left another man at the altar.

She said herself she was commitment-shy.

What if he asked her to marry him, she agreed, and then she left him at the altar, too? The same way she had her former fiancé?

That possibility was like a cold, glaring light turned on in the middle of his rosy fantasy.

Unfortunately he had experience with being deserted by a woman. And he knew for a certainty that no amount of love could keep anyone from taking off if she had a mind to—for whatever reason.

Ivey might not be anything like his ex-wife, but the end result could well be the same. He could get himself in hook, line and sinker, get his kids into it, too, and then be left behind. Hurting again. With two little girls crying for yet another woman who hadn't been able to stick around....

Damn.

How could he risk putting his kids through that again?

How could he risk putting himself through that again?

Cully broke into a cold sweat just thinking about it.

He wanted to believe Ivey wouldn't leave him hanging the way Kim had because she was so different from Kim. But like Kim or not like Kim, there was no denying that Ivey had gotten cold feet just as she was on the verge of marrying that other guy and run off. And no matter how big a creep her former fiancé was, Cully was worried about what Ivey's actions said about her ability to make and follow through with a commitment. Trying to include her in his and the girls' lives permanently seemed like taking a risk. A big risk. Maybe a huge one.

And he just couldn't take that risk.

He loved Ivey. There was no denying that. And he wanted her in the worst way. But the worst way was that he—and Amy and Randa—were likely to be left high and dry if he tried to bring her into their family.

And that was just not something he could put any of them through again.

With his arms still tightly around Ivey, he kissed the top of her head, lingering there with his eyes pinched shut, wishing to God things could be different.

But he knew they couldn't be. And he had to force himself to accept it just the way he'd had to learn to accept things with Kim.

He loosened his hold of Ivey and slipped out of her bed.

The hint of daybreak let soft pink light creep in through the window to fall across her face as she slept on.

Cully dressed soundlessly, watching her the whole time.

He couldn't have loved her more. He couldn't have wanted her more. It was an ache inside him, as if he'd been sucker punched. And not getting back in bed, not pulling her into his arms again, not making love to her, not trying to find a way to keep her with him forever, was the hardest thing he'd ever done in all of his thirty-five years.

But once before he'd done his damnedest to hang on to a woman who didn't want to be hung on to and he knew as surely as Ivey's former fiancé knew now that it didn't work. That when a woman couldn't make that commitment, she couldn't make that commitment.

So he didn't do anything but stand there and watch her sleep for a few minutes more.

Then he whispered a soft, "Goodbye, Ivey," and went silently out of her room, out of her house, out of her life, as if staying anywhere near her any longer might weaken his will and make him forget what he knew he had to do—put distance between them.

Fast.

Before he couldn't put distance between them at all and he ended up laying himself, his heart, his kids on the line yet again, only to have *her* put the distance between them all when they least expected it.

Ivey wasn't sure what woke her. She just knew that suddenly something wasn't right. It took her a little while to come fully awake and realize what it was. To remember that Cully had been in bed with her, big and warm beside her, holding her.

And when she recalled that, she recalled everything. Coming home from the Harvest Festival dance. Making love. Falling asleep on top of Cully after that first time. Waking to make love again. Then sleeping once more curled up against him, her head on his chest, his powerful arms around her....

But now he was gone.

She reached over to where he'd been before, feeling the heat of his body just as she heard his truck engine start up outside.

So he hadn't just gone to the bathroom, she thought, and a wave of bad feelings washed through her all of a sudden. A wave that got even worse when she heard him peel away from the front of her house as if he couldn't wait to escape from here. From her.

She opened her eyes, sat up in bed pulling the covers with her to hold across her bare breasts, and turned on the bedside lamp.

The time on her clock radio was 5:53 a.m. The sun was only beginning to make an appearance outside. And nowhere in the room was there a sign that Cully had even been there.

Or so much as a note to say why he'd left the way he had. Like a thief in the night.

It jarred Ivey.

Cully was only the second man she'd ever been intimate with. That wasn't something she took lightly. It meant something to her. But it occurred to her right then that it wasn't such a big deal to him and that stabbed her like a knife.

Why hadn't he awakened her to say he was leaving?

Why hadn't he given her a few moments with him before he was gone?

Just a few moments to put a proper, respectful, caring ending to what had happened between them the night before. To making love. A few moments to confirm that she hadn't imagined the closeness they'd shared. To let her know he'd meant it when he'd said he loved her. That she wasn't just an evening's entertainment...

But he hadn't given her those few moments and that omission bruised her heart. And her pride.

Was it possible this had only been a one-night stand to him? A roll in the hay?

Because lying there alone now, feeling as if there hadn't been any closure to what they'd opened up the previous night, made it seem that way to her. It made it seem as if none of what they'd done, none of what they'd said, had really mattered very much to him.

Love 'em and leave 'em...

She'd heard someone say that was what the Culhanes did. Sure, it had been a long time ago. In a bathroom when she was in high school, when all the Culhanes were mere boys. Said by someone who'd had an encounter with one or another of them—Ivey couldn't even remember which one.

But now those words rang in her ears. Is that what Cully had done? Loved her and left her? Literally and figuratively?

She didn't want to believe it but she couldn't help it. A few hours of passion and he was out the door. Without so much as a thank-you-ma'am...

Ivey clamped her eyes closed and slid farther under the covers again, groaning miserably as she did.

Had she done it again? she asked herself. Had she

misjudged yet another man? Taken him to be something he wasn't? Overlooked some awful character flaw?

She was terrified that she had. That she'd chosen poorly again.

But then what did she expect when she'd made that choice in such a haze of emotion? Ruled by the overpowering attraction she'd felt for Cully? When she'd let that guide her? Interfere with her thinking?

Surely Cully hadn't been operating under that same haze of emotion or he would have still been in bed with her now, saying a tender farewell even if he did have to get home, making plans for when they could be together again, for where their relationship might go from here....

"Maybe this really was a wake-up call," she said to herself. Not from sleep, but from what was happening between her and Cully. A wake-up call to let her know things weren't the way they seemed to her. That Cully wasn't who he seemed to be.

But at least she'd had her eyes opened before it was too late this time, she thought. Before she got all the way to a wedding.

She just couldn't read men, that's all there was to it, and she'd better learn to act accordingly. To deal with it.

Maybe it was better if she just stayed away from them. Completely away from them. Where she was safe. Safe from the abuse of men like Arlen. Safe from falling so deeply, intensely, passionately in love with men like Cully. So deeply, intensely, passionately in love that she could hardly breathe for how much it hurt when they left her like this.

And it did hurt. So, so much...

Enough to leave an indelible mark.

And to leave a new strength in her to keep the vow she made not to let it happen again.

No matter what.

"Man! Who put the burr under your saddle today?" Clint asked Cully at the end of the afternoon as the three brothers headed for the house they shared. "You didn't need to jump all over that stable boy. He's new. He probably just didn't know where those tacks go."

Cully didn't answer that. He just gave Clint a warning glare.

"Seems like spendin' the whole night over at Ivey Heller's place you'd be in a good temper, not a bad one," Yance chimed in. "What the hell happened over there to make you so contrary?"

Cully was on the verge of telling his brothers to mind their own damn business, keep their own damn opinions to themselves. But he'd been in a lousy mood since leaving Ivey's house at dawn, and barking at everyone—which he'd been doing plenty of all day long—hadn't helped so far.

So he decided to tell them what was on his mind, that his night with Ivey had been good enough to make him want a whole lifetime of them, but why he couldn't try for that.

Both Clint and Yance had stuck close by through Cully's divorce; they knew what he'd been through and neither of them took lightly what he confided in them as he laid it all out.

"Better off steerin' clear of a woman who can't keep her word, all right," Clint agreed as they stood around the kitchen by the end of the story, each with a beer in hand.

"That's what I figured," Cully confirmed, staring morosely at the bottle he held. "But I don't like it."

"Nothin' to like about gettin' deserted either, though," Yance reminded.

The three of them fell into a silence that Cully took for agreement. And ratification. They were all of a like mind: he'd done the right thing by leaving Ivey this morning. By figuring on that being the end of any relationship with her.

"On the other hand," Clint reasoned suddenly, "from what you and the girls said about that guy Ivey was goin' to marry, sounds like she was smart to get away from him."

"And what about Ivey herself?" Yance asked. "It wasn't just you and the kids Kim couldn't stick with. She couldn't stick with anything. Is Ivey like that, too? Or was it just that she dumped some jackass who deserved to be left waitin' at the altar?"

The phone rang right then, before Cully could answer his brothers or even think about what they'd said.

Yance picked it up because he was the closest and the tone of his end of the conversation made both Cully and Clint redirect their attention to what was being said.

"No. You're jokin'," Yance muttered, sounding ominous. "Can't be..."

It went on like that for a while before he said goodbye, replaced the receiver and turned a somber expression to them. But for a moment he just stared into space, shaking his head in what looked like disbelief, as if he couldn't grasp what he'd heard from the other end.

"What was that about?" Clint asked.

"Bucky Dennehy," Yance finally said. "He had a heart attack over at the radio station. He's dead."

"Holy mother... He can't be dead. He's only your age, Yance." This from Clint.

"My age or not, he was gone before the doc could cross the street and get to him. Looks like a massive coronary."

"God. And there's Della and those four little kids..." Cully said, thinking out loud more than anything.

The three of them stood there in solemn silence for a time, letting the news sink in. Bucky Dennehy was more than just another face in town. He was a friend. They'd grown up together. Raised hell together before they'd all settled down. Partied, played, worked, celebrated together ever since.

"I guess you never know what's waiting around the next corner," Cully said.

"So maybe you better not turn up your nose at what you can have today just because of what might happen tomorrow, huh?" Yance mused, aiming it at Cully, but his tone only presenting it hypothetically, as something maybe Cully should consider.

But now didn't seem like the time for anything to do with Cully's problems and Clint and Yance both drifted out of the kitchen, murmuring their intention to shower and get into town, see if there was anything they could do for the family.

Cully had Amy and Randa to see to, to feed dinner when they came in any minute now from staying with the daughter of their ranch foreman who'd been baby-sitting today, so he was left with nothing but his thoughts.

Bucky Dennehy dead.

It kept going through Cully's mind over and over again, no easier to believe than when he'd first heard it.

No one really did know what was in store for them, he began to think.

Did that mean Yance was right? Should he not turn his nose up at what he could have with Ivey now just because of what *might* happen in the future?

It was tempting to use that to throw caution to the wind, as an excuse to go to Ivey the way he wanted to, the way he'd wanted to all day long.

But just because fate could reach out a hand and pluck somebody off the earth on a whim didn't mean a person should go blindly, foolishly through the days leading up to it, he told himself.

Yet something else his brothers had said before the phone call came back to mind as he stood there pondering it all.

Ivey's fiancé had been a real horse's patooty. Cully had seen it with his own eyes. Hell, he'd had to pull the bastard off her. Seemed smart to run out on marrying that guy, not commitment-shy the way Ivey had said.

So what about Yance's earlier suggestion to look at Ivey herself, to remember what Kim had been like in comparison?

Nothing else about Ivey gave any indication that she had problems sticking with things. Savannah had said she and Ivey had lived in that small apartment since they'd graduated from college, that even though they could afford a bigger, better place, they stayed anyway because they were attached to it. Savannah had even joked that she'd been worried Ivey hadn't gone through with the wedding because it was too big a change for her. Hadn't he said himself that Ivey must not have much of a wandering spirit to her because of it?

And what about coming back to Elk Creek? When Ivey had needed to make a change in where she was living—even only a temporary one—it had been to home base, to familiar turf, to a place where it wasn't a change to anything new or unknown. And it wasn't because she'd grown bored with where she was or what she was doing.

Then there was her car, Cully thought. A ten-year-old relic she kept because she couldn't bear to part with it, she'd told him that herself.

And her job—she'd stayed with the same job for years and years. That was why she could take this time off now, she'd said.

Were these indications of someone who couldn't make a commitment and keep it? He didn't see how.

Plus, when he thought about his ex-wife in the same scenarios he knew for a fact that she couldn't have done any of what Ivey had. She would have moved two dozen times, driven as many different cars, and she certainly wouldn't have—*couldn't* have—stuck with the same job all that time.

And something else occurred to Cully just then.

Ivey had admitted that she hadn't loved her fiancé the way she knew she needed to to marry him. What had she said? He didn't make her hear bells and whistles. That, coupled with the kind of person he was, seemed like two big—*really* big—reasons not to go through with marrying him.

Commitment-shy? Suddenly Cully just couldn't see it, no matter what Ivey had said.

Maybe he was fooling himself, but whether she'd

said it or not, he just didn't believe that a single act made a person commitment-shy.

Or a bad risk.

Not when so many other things spoke differently about her.

But even if there was a touch of a commitment problem lurking beneath the surface, what was his alternative to not at least talking to her, asking her about all this? To finding out if she felt the bells-and-whistles kind of love for him?

The alternative was not having her in his life. Losing her right now, without so much as an attempt to work it out.

And he couldn't stand that thought. He hadn't been able to stand it all day long—that was why he'd been biting everybody's head off. Now, considering Bucky's death and the reminder of just how tenuous life could be, and how important it was to grab for what he wanted with both hands while he still could, it seemed all the more important not to give up without a try.

He loved Ivey, He wanted her. He thought she was going to an extreme to call herself commitment-shy over leaving her creep of a fiancé at the altar. He could only hope she was hearing bells and whistles when they were together.

But he wouldn't know any of that for sure unless he went over there, saw her again, hashed through it all.

Unless he gave them both a chance...

Ivey could see someone sitting on her porch steps as she drove up to the house about nine that night. Only the glow of the moon illuminated him, but there was no mistaking Cully, even if she hadn't recognized his truck parked not far from where he sat.

Her immediate response was a warm elation at knowing he was there, that she could come back from the grief of Della's house to the comfort of Cully, of his arms, of being with him rather than being alone at a time when she really didn't want to be.

Then she remembered how this day had begun, the long, empty hours she'd spent hoping he'd call or come over and make everything all right, and her feelings were instantly tinged with a new grief of her own.

"Been over to see Della?" he asked as she got out of her car and headed for the house.

"Since I heard about Bucky a little while ago."

"How's she doin'?"

"Bad. Things are real bad there. But Linc and Kansas are staying with her and the kids. The doctor gave her something to make her sleep and cleared everyone else out."

"Terrible, terrible thing. I still can't believe Bucky's gone."

Ivey couldn't add anything to that. And she didn't want to sit cozily beside Cully on the porch steps as if nothing were wrong between them. Or even invite him inside, afraid that her will would weaken, and she'd give in to her feelings for him, the comfort only he could offer. So she just climbed the stairs without saying more, crossed the porch and unlocked the front door.

But Cully wasn't waiting for an invitation. By the time she'd done that he was behind her, holding the screen door, following her in as if he had the right to.

"I don't think I'm up for company," she said coolly as she set her purse and keys on the hall table, not turning to look at him.

"Mad at me, are you?" he guessed, a recoil in his voice as if she'd lashed out physically.

"Not exactly mad. Disappointed. Disillusioned. Surprised at you..." And hurt. Very, very hurt.

But she didn't add that. She didn't want him to know just how much he'd hurt her.

"Lousy way for me to leave things this mornin'," he guessed again.

"Lousy way for you to leave me," she amended, the hurt creeping into her voice anyway.

"Want to know why I did?"

"I don't think it matters as much why as that you did. That it was something I wouldn't have thought you would do."

"Ouch."

She couldn't stay with her back to him forever, looking down at the hall table rather than at him. So she shored herself up with a mental stroll through all the misery she'd suffered today and finally turned around, leaning against the table for support and making it clear she wasn't going to be friendly enough to let him get any farther than the entryway.

But shored up or not, one look at his sculpted face and she nearly crumbled. Nearly closed the few feet of distance that separated them and slipped into his arms the way her body cried out for her to.

To keep herself from doing that she clamped both hands to the table's edge on either side of her hips and held on tight.

"I don't know if you'll believe this or not," he said then, "but when I woke up this morning it was with the intention of askin' you to marry me."

"Were you thinking of mailing it in?"

He did a wry little chuckle at that, as if accepting

that he had the sarcasm coming. But he didn't answer it. Instead he said, "Then I started worryin'. About how you'd left that other guy at the altar. About how you said yourself you were commitment-shy. About bein' left behind the way I was once before..." He shook his head. "Seemed like I'd be askin' for a whole lot of heartache. For myself and for Amy and Randa."

"So you hightailed it out of here," she finished saying for him, none too nicely.

"Ooo, you really are ticked off at me," he said with a frown that beetled his brow.

"Actually I'm a lot more ticked off at me."

"I've been feelin' that way myself all day and all through tonight, waitin' for Yance and Clint to come home and baby-sit for the kids so I could get over here."

"You were ticked off at me, too?"

"At myself. For not seein' some things before. For takin' things at face value."

"Not a good idea," she said, since taking things at face value was what had gotten her into so much trouble twice now. "It's better to look beyond the surface. Deeper. To what's really there. If you can find it."

He frowned again at the pointedness with which she said that but didn't address it. Instead he went on to explain all the things he'd thought about her today, all he'd come to realize about her, to believe about her.

"Not going through with that wedding was a single act," he said as he finished up. "And no single act makes you commitment-shy, Ivey. Believe me, I've had experience with someone who really was commitment-shy and you don't have any of the symptoms. But you announced it to me and it stuck. It didn't occur to me until tonight that you were exaggerating. Hell, I don't think it's occurred to *you* that saying you were commitment-shy was an exaggeration. A false accusation, really, that doesn't fit you or what you did. Still, though, I accepted it at face value and—''

''Took off.''

''And decided not to ask for a commitment from someone else who couldn't give it.''

He moved slightly closer to her but she must not have seemed too open to the idea because he stopped halfway there, shifted his weight onto one leg and bracketed his hips with his hands, looking altogether too sexy for her own good.

Ivey tried not to notice. Fighting her feelings for him, her attraction to him, the whole time.

''It may have come a little late, but I know damn well that you're not someone who can't make or keep a commitment, Ivey,'' he went on. ''So I had to get over here tonight to tell you that I love you, that I loved last night and I want a million more of them. And I want to ask you what I wanted to ask you in bed this mornin'—will you marry me?''

She stood there staring at him. Staring hard. She wanted to say yes, she'd marry him. Because she did want to marry him. At least she wanted to marry the man she'd thought she went to bed with the previous night.

But somehow the words wouldn't come out. Because now she wasn't so sure he was the man she'd thought he was then.

She couldn't help wondering what was going on behind that great face of his. She couldn't help thinking that this morning, when she'd been sleeping peacefully in his arms, sure that everything between them was perfect, he'd been thinking about how *imperfect* she was. He'd been convincing himself that he shouldn't propose, that she was too flawed to invite into his life. He'd been finding fault the same way Arlen had always found fault.

Did that make him like Arlen? she asked herself.

Until today she'd have said absolutely not.

But then, early in her relationship with Arlen she would have said Arlen was nothing like he proved to be, either.

She just didn't know. She just couldn't trust her own judgment. Not when she'd been so wrong about Arlen before, not when all she'd been able to think about since this morning was how wrong she might have been again, about Cully. That once more something very different had been going on inside a man's head than what she'd thought.

It left her too afraid at that moment to trust herself. To trust him. Too afraid to agree to yet another marriage to yet another man who could well prove to be not the man she thought he was. Who could well prove to be the kind of man who would be secretly finding fault in her when she least expected it. Who could leave her at moments when she was sure he'd be there for her.

"I keep thinking that it's a very real possibility that I don't actually know you," she murmured, more to herself than to him.

"What do you mean you don't know me? You've known me all your life."

She just shook her head. "Face value," she repeated. "I know what's on the outside. Not what's on the inside."

"What do you want me to do? I'd turn myself inside

out if I thought that would help. But all you'd see is a man who loves you.''

But she suddenly didn't feel so sure of that, either. Would a man who truly loved her have left the way he had this morning? Would he have doubted her so severely? Would he have hurt her?

Ivey just went on staring at him, trying hard to see beyond the surface, to find a way to trust her own judgment, the judgment that had failed her so terribly in the past....

"Marry me, Ivey," Cully coaxed.

Again she shook her head. Not as a refusal of his proposal, but ruminatively, as a way of saying she just didn't know if she could, that she just wasn't sure....

But he took it as a refusal. "Dammit! I don't know how to convince you that what you see is what you'd get. All I can tell you is the same thing my brother told me—take a look at what you know about me, what you've seen in my actions."

"Actions like leaving this morning without so much as a 'Have a nice day'?"

"A single act, Ivey. Remember that. It was a single act. Like your running out on your wedding. Weigh it against the rest of what you know about me. Then make a decision."

He met her eyes with his ice blue ones then, held them captive for a few moments as if to let her see into his soul.

But after those few moments had passed he turned without saying any more and went out of the house, back to his truck.

And once again Ivey listened to him drive away, this time not with the urgency she'd heard this morning.

But even so she was a little surprised to find herself

suddenly alone, left with nothing but an emotional homework assignment from him.

And feeling no less hurt and confused than she had been since opening her eyes at dawn.

Chapter Ten

Nearly all of Elk Creek closed down for Bucky Dennehy's funeral and almost the whole town attended. It was a terribly sad occasion and Ivey's heart went out to Della and her four small children, who all looked as if they didn't quite believe what had happened even as they stared at the grave site. Della's and Kansas's parents stood on one side of them, Bucky's family on the other, and Kansas and Linc were directly behind them, all offering what they could in the way of support. But nothing changed the lost, bereft look in each of their eyes.

Savannah had come home to the small town only that morning for the services and to be with her friend, though Della seemed to be in such a state of shock that Ivey wasn't sure she was even aware of it.

But for her part, Ivey was glad to have her sister

there. It helped not to be alone when she was anywhere near Cully.

It wasn't easy to see him, to wish he was by her side, to want to be going through this with him. Not when she needed to keep her distance from him.

But she knew she couldn't make a clearheaded decision if she didn't keep that distance from him; otherwise she'd give in to the power of her attraction for him, to loving him even as she worried she shouldn't. Having Savannah with her gave her the stamina she needed to stay away.

A church group was overseeing a buffet at Della's house after the interment but as mourners filed away from the graveside to the waiting cars and trucks, and Savannah had a few words with Kansas and Linc, Ivey wandered away to a spot she hadn't visited in fifteen years—the spot where her father was buried.

The cemetery was well kept up so Silas's headstone was clean and the grass was trim over the grave itself. But just in front of the stone, a thorny thistle weed was beginning to sprout.

Ivey knelt down and picked it, catching sight of her sister's shoes as Savannah joined her.

She half expected her sister to make a comment about how apt it was that a thorny thistle weed was growing from the grave of someone who'd been a thorny thistle of a man, but Savannah didn't address it at all. Instead she said, "So talk to me."

Ivey stood again, weed in hand, and said, "Who? Me or Dad?"

"You. What's going on between you and Cully Culhane? First you were getting crazier and crazier about him by the minute. Now I find you avoiding him like the plague, sneaking long looks at him when you think he won't notice. Something's up. So let's have it.''

"He asked me to marry him," Ivey said, surprising her sister with the news, if Savannah's expression was any indication.

"You don't look like a happily engaged couple."

"Maybe that's because we aren't happy or engaged.''

Standing there in the cemetery, Ivey told her sister the whole story, leaving nothing out and almost expecting their father's voice to come from beyond the grave to tell her she was an idiot, a stupid romantic fool for even entertaining notions about Cully.

But of course that didn't happen and when she was finished Savannah said, "Oh, Ivey," in a way that was almost a moan.

"*Oh, Ivey* what?"

"Sometimes you're as bad as Silas was."

"I beg your pardon."

"He was hard as nails on us and you're keeping up the tradition by being hard as nails on yourself. Running out on that wedding was not the worst thing you could ever have done. I don't know if what's happened between you and Cully Culhane is good or not but I do know he's right that a single act isn't the be-all and end-all of the world.''

"But, Savannah—"

"No buts about it. Sure you were afraid of spending the rest of your life with Arlen. But not because of the commitment. Because you'd realized he was a jerk and that you didn't love him. That doesn't mean you were commitment-shy then and it certainly doesn't mean you will be in the future. Cully Culhane has it pegged— you do just fine at making and keeping commitments.

I see you doing it all the time. In your work. In the way we live. In everything. What else do you call sticking with the same job all these years? Driving the same car? Living in the same place—just the way Cully said?"

"Commitment," Ivey conceded.

"And you didn't miss early on that Arlen was a jerk because you're a bad judge of men. You missed it because he hid it from you. He played Mr. Charm, Mr. Nice Guy, Mr. Lovable, until he had you where he wanted you and then he let his true colors show. He was just cunning enough to camouflage his flaws until it was almost too late. *I* thought he was a decent person until the last few months when he started being himself. Do you think I have bad judgment?"

Ivey knew better than that and it made her laugh slightly at the very suggestion that Savannah might misjudge anyone.

"I can't tell you what to do with Cully Culhane and his proposal," Savannah went on. "I can't tell you if you're right or wrong about him maybe not being the man you thought he was before the other morning or whether running out after a night of lovemaking was a sign of *his* true colors. That's something you have to decide for yourself. But I do know he's right about these other things, that you've gone to extremes condemning yourself when there was no reason for it. Let it all go. And definitely stop questioning your judgment now so you can put it to work."

"I have been taking things to extremes," Ivey agreed. "I was even searching for signs that Cully was just like Dad because he's a man left alone with two daughters by a woman who ran off the way Mom did. And because he doesn't dress his girls in frilly things and he fosters them being little tomboys. I was so sure being a hard, cold—'' she held up the weed and laughed slightly again ''—thorny thistle of a man was going to come out that I was just waiting for it, almost baiting him.''

''And did it?''

''No. Never.'' And really, Savannah was probably right that condemning herself as commitment-shy and having poor judgment of men over just one incident, one man, was part of going to those extremes.

But what about Cully? Was he what he seemed? Could she trust her earlier impressions of him? Her feelings for him?

She just didn't know.

''Come on,'' Savannah said into her thoughts, interrupting them before Ivey had any answers. ''I can see Della still at Bucky's grave, all by herself, and she doesn't look too good. I think we better go over to her.''

The reminder of Della made Ivey's own problems seem minor so she put them aside and crossed the cemetery with her sister.

Della was standing dry-eyed, staring at the flower-draped casket where it hovered over a tarp-covered grave.

''Della?'' Savannah said softly as they approached. ''Are you okay?''

Della shook her head, not moving her eyes from the coffin. ''I said I wanted to have a last few minutes alone with him, but the truth is that I feel like I can't leave. Like if I do, he really will be dead.''

''Oh, honey,'' Savannah breathed sympathetically, putting her arm around her friend's shoulders, clearly not knowing what else to say or do.

"I know—I can't stay here," Della said reasonably, tears falling down her cheeks suddenly. "And it wouldn't make any difference if I did. It wouldn't bring him back. But I just can't make myself leave."

Savannah squeezed the other woman's shoulders and joked gently, "Do you want *me* to make you leave?"

Della managed a small laugh at that. "Maybe you better."

"Okay then, come on," Savannah said with mock firmness.

Della took a deep breath, pressed her fingertips to her lips then touched them to the mahogany coffin for one last moment while huge tears flooded her eyes again.

"Goodbye, Bucky," she whispered very, very quietly, in an agony of grief that filled the air around them even without any volume to her voice.

Then she turned away, heading for the mortuary car that waited for her, with Savannah still hugging her shoulders and Ivey closing ranks on her other side.

"I can't ride in that thing," she said of the funeral limousine that seemed to loom there ahead of them. "Will you guys take me home?"

"You know we will," Ivey assured, sending Savannah and Della to get into her small sedan while she went to let the limousine driver know he could go.

By the time Ivey made it to her car Savannah was in the back seat and Della was in the passenger seat, blowing her nose and mopping her face as if she had things under control. For the time being anyway.

"So what's this about you and Cully Culhane being inseparable since you've been back?" she said to Ivey as Ivey started the engine, sounding only remotely interested and obviously just trying hard to distract herself from her own grief in whatever way provided itself.

"We were seeing a lot of each other," Ivey confirmed.

"But you aren't now?"

"No."

"She's trying to figure out if he's one of the good guys or one of the bad guys," Savannah interjected from the rear.

"He's one of the good guys," Della said without missing a beat. "I see pretty much of him because of the kids—his and mine are in some of the same play groups, go to the same parties, sometimes just want to get together. He's definitely one of the good guys. A good man. A good father…"

That started the tears again as Della's voice trailed off but she blew her nose once more, obviously fighting to stop them.

When she had a semblance of control again she said, "Do you love him?"

"Yes," Ivey answered without having to think about it.

"Then you better not let him go, Ivey," Della said as if it were the most important thing she'd said in a long, long time. "Don't let that love or that man out of your grasp. Do you see how short life is? How easy it is to lose what you think will just be there waiting forever? Don't waste time. And don't waste that love.…"

The crying started again at the same moment Ivey pulled into the driveway of Della's house—the only spot for blocks and blocks that wasn't already taken up by the same cars and trucks that had been at the cemetery.

"I mean it," Della said through her tears, ignoring the fact that they'd arrived home and a number of caring people were watching them from inside the house and from outside on the lawn. "If you love him and he loves you, everything else can be worked out. Especially if all you're worried about is that he isn't a good man. Because he is."

Della struggled with her tears yet again, drying her eyes, blowing her nose. Then she seemed to see for the first time all the people who were waiting for her and she got out of the car, closing the door behind her.

"Poor Della," Ivey said softly, thinking that much of what she'd said came from her own feelings of loss.

"She's in a bad way, all right," Savannah agreed. "But she could be right anyhow."

Savannah got out of the car to follow Della, and Ivey trailed behind them.

She didn't want to be on the lookout for Cully as she went into the house but she was. Not that she didn't still keep her distance once she located him because she did, maintaining it even as she kept track of his whereabouts surreptitiously.

He stayed with the rest of the men who mainly huddled in groups, leaving the lion's share of the condolence giving to the women.

But just as Savannah had observed earlier, Ivey cast Cully long glances when he seemed not to be looking, wondering about him the whole while.

If she conceded that commitment problems and poor judgment were not real issues to keep her away from him, then that left only Cully himself. And his silent faultfinding when she thought everything between them was going well. And his leaving her without a word the morning after making love to her. And whether or not he was the man she'd thought him to be before that.

Was there a darker side to him, the way there had been to Arlen?

Della didn't think so.

But what did Ivey herself know about him?

She knew he was a good father. That in spite of having tried to find flaws in his parenting, in spite of trying to peg him as the kind of father her own had been, he'd come through with flying colors. His daughters adored him and he didn't try to pigeonhole them in any way she could see. Or make them into boys he would rather have had.

No, he delighted in them and they delighted in him.

She also recognized the fact that he hadn't shirked his responsibilities to them when his wife had left. That rather than turning the kids over to some other relative to raise or forcing their mother to take them, or even just pawning them off on a nanny or baby-sitters so he didn't have to bother with them, he'd plunged into being a single father, juggling that with the demands of running a ranch and not slighting Amy or Randa in any way Ivey had seen.

And what about the man himself?

He'd come to her rescue with Arlen, stepping into the middle of the fray without being asked to. And then he'd made sure she was locked in safe and sound, and knew she could call on him if Arlen showed up again.

Those weren't signs of a bad person. A chivalrous one. A gallant one. A brave one. A protective, caring, concerned one. But not a bad one.

There was also his help cleaning the house up when she'd first gotten here. His refusal to be paid for it because in his book one neighbor helping another was not something he would accept money to do. Even the arrangement for her baby-sitting in return had seemed to be more to humor her than as any kind of remuneration.

Ethics. Integrity. Generosity. All good things. Things that didn't lend weight to him harboring a mean spirit or a bad character.

And what about the way Cully had treated her as a woman?

There hadn't been any put-downs. No criticisms. Not once had he reminded her of her father, which couldn't be said of Arlen. And not once had Cully reminded her of Arlen, either.

No, Cully had treated her with respect, with kindness, with admiration for her intelligence, for what she did for a living.

His only mistake had been that morning after...

A single act.

Did she believe the reasons he'd given for it?

He'd been deserted by a woman who couldn't make a commitment, left holding the bag, hurt by the abandonment. Was it so hard to understand that he would be especially leery of getting involved with a woman who'd come in announcing she was commitment-shy? Was it so hard to understand his worrying about protecting himself, his kids, from the same kind of pain his ex-wife had inflicted on them all?

No, it wasn't hard to believe or understand.

And in truth, it was more of an indication that he was a good father in that he was trying to do what was best for his daughters yet again.

A single act...

The same way the single act of leaving Arlen at the altar didn't mean she was commitment-shy, maybe the

single act of Cully doubting her, of leaving her high
and dry after a night of lovemaking shouldn't condemn
him. Shouldn't totally wipe away the good she *did*
know about him. It shouldn't make her think she'd misjudged him, that the rest of what she knew about him
for a fact should be wiped out, that she should think
he wasn't the man she'd thought him to be.

And to top it all off, there was Della's endorsement.
Ivey didn't discount that. Della had lived in Elk Creek
all these years with Cully. Known him. Watched him.
And she'd said—with force—that he was a good man.

A good man. Maybe one of the best.

And certainly the only one Ivey loved. With all her
heart. Truly, truly loved in a way that told her without
a doubt that she'd never really loved Arlen. That she'd
been fooling herself early on to consider what she'd
felt for him genuine love.

And Cully was the only man she wanted to marry.
To have babies with. To spend the rest of her life with.

No, she didn't have commitment problems, she realized just then. Because the idea of till death do we
part with Cully didn't scare her in the least, let alone
panic her the way it had with Arlen. Instead it was a
very appealing proposition.

Till death do we part...

Poor Della...

But Della was right about something else, too, Ivey
thought. She was right about not letting love, not letting
Cully, get away. That life was too short not to grab on
to what she and Cully could have together.

If only she wasn't too late. If only she hadn't already
wasted too much time...

Ivey felt that Della's house was not the place to tell
Cully that she'd done her emotional homework, that

she loved him, wanted him. So she went on keeping her distance from him the whole time she was there.

By early evening the crowd started to dwindle and since Savannah had offered to spend the night with Della, Ivey left by herself.

Both evenings since Cully had proposed to Ivey he'd shown up at her place to tend the animals in her barn. He hadn't come near the house. He hadn't bothered Ivey at all. But she'd known the minute he'd arrived and the minute he'd left and she'd been hard put not to watch for him at her kitchen window in between.

Tonight she positioned herself at her bedroom window instead because from the second floor she could see farther so she'd know when he was headed her way.

If he came.

If he didn't she wasn't sure what she'd do. If she'd go to his house or not. She just hoped she wouldn't have to. That this could be done in the privacy of her place.

It was after seven when she finally spotted him. Riding in on horseback. Sitting tall and straight in the saddle. Dressed in blue jeans and the white western shirt he'd worn under his suit to the funeral, almost glowing fluorescent in the milky light of the moon.

His head was bare of the Stetson he wore to block the sun in the daytime and that same moonlight kissed the top of his sable brown hair and only the high points of his starkly masculine, handsome features. But it was enough to make her heart skip a beat.

She watched him until he was inside the barn before she came away from the window and made a quick trip to the bathroom in the hall to check the way she looked. She gave her curly hair an unnecessary fluff to enliven the loose mass, made sure her red V-neck T-shirt was tucked tightly into her black jeans, and then pinched her cheeks to add a little color because even through her makeup she looked pale.

But she didn't dawdle longer than that, afraid that if she did Cully might leave before she got down to him.

She left the house silently and slipped into the barn through the open great door the same way. But once she was inside she closed it behind her, letting that sound announce her.

"Ivey?" Cully's deep, rich voice came from behind her, sounding as if he wasn't sure it was her.

"Hi," she answered simply enough as she turned to face him, finding him in the center aisle just outside one of the stalls, looking gorgeous and slightly troubled, as if he thought she might be bringing bad news.

"Somethin' wrong?" he asked.

"Not anymore. At least I hope not anymore," she answered as she headed in his direction.

"Did some thinkin', did you?" he said, watching her come, his ice blue eyes taking in every curve from head to toe and back again, his expression easing up.

"A lot of thinking," she confirmed.

"About you and me?"

"And Arlen and my father and Della and Bucky Dennehy."

He nodded as if her thinking about all those other people in conjunction with him was only normal. "And what did you come up with?"

She told him. Every bit of it. And he listened raptly, leaning one broad shoulder against an end post, crossing his arms over his chest and his right ankle over his left, keeping his eyes on her every minute.

"Looks to me like we're two fruitcakes for lettin' old business interfere with new," he said when she'd finished.

"But at least we were smart enough to realize it and get past it."

"Are you past it?" he asked very seriously.

"I know now that I'm not commitment-shy and that my judgment in men was less faulty than the man himself. And that I was right not to marry him. And I know I can forgive your worrying about how what I told you was a commitment problem would impact you and your kids. And that I can even forgive your running out on the morning after we made love for the first time...so long as it never—and I mean *never*—happens again."

"The making love or the running out?" he teased.

"The running out."

His supple lips eased into a half grin. "Does that mean I'm goin' to get the chance to make love to you again?"

"Maybe," she said coyly when what she was thinking was *many, many times, if only you still want to...*

He pushed off the post with his shoulder and closed the gap between them, coming to stand directly in front of her but not touching her. "Does it mean you're going to let me put a ring on your finger to do it?"

"Depends on the kind of ring you were thinking about."

"The kind that ropes you, ties you up and brands you as mine forever."

"Sounds painful," she joked.

"I hope it won't be," he joked back. Then he sobered somewhat. "Will you marry me, Ivey?"

"And be your wife till death do we part?"

"At least."

"Yes."

"That's it?" he said with a tinge of disbelief. "No qualms? No conditions?"

"No qualms. No panic attacks at the thought of forever. Nothing."

Cully reached for her then, pulling her into his arms where he kissed her—tenderly, sweetly, with passion peeking in from around the edges.

But that passion couldn't stay around the edges for long. Not now, when everything had been resolved between them. When they were both free of all the barriers that had complicated things, all the inhibitions that had come with them.

Their kisses grew hungry, urgent. Hands that at first seemed only to seek reassurance that they really were together again began instead to explore. To arouse. To possess as each had given the other the right to do.

It flashed through Ivey's thoughts that this was literally a roll in the hay, but it only made her smile as Cully swept her up into his arms and laid her down on a bed of the freshly cut stuff covered by a blanket he'd pulled down from the stall wall.

They both made quick work of shedding clothes that were only obstacles to what they needed, wanted, leaving them unhindered as he kissed a path down to her breasts, reveling in her body as she boldly reveled in his. Every caress cherished, pleased, excited, and neither of them could keep from moaning in turn.

They made love right there in the barn. Staking their claim. Sealing it. Laughing and teasing and blissfully tormenting in a way that shouted that this was only a beginning for them. A beginning that climaxed in an explosion of ecstasy that left Ivey clinging to Cully's broad back, that left Cully plunging so deeply into her she thought he really had touched her heart, an ecstasy that left them gloriously spent and one truly a part of the other.

"I love you, Ivey," Cully said softly.

"I love you, too."

"But I'm not kiddin' when I say I want a whole lifetime with you," he warned.

"Good, because that's what I'm planning on."

He kissed her again and then just held her so tight their bodies were almost melded into one, pressing her head to his hard chest, resting his chin in the nest of her hair.

"Hear that?" he asked in a hushed voice as if to speak louder would drown something out.

"Bells and whistles?" she guessed with a laugh.

"They're loud and clear to me."

"To me, too," she said, feeling happy tears well up in her eyes.

Cully sighed then, a sigh of relief as if he hadn't been too sure things were going to end this way and he'd been on pins and needles worrying about it.

But he didn't need to worry anymore. Not about her. Certainly not about her running out on their wedding.

Because unlike the last time, she didn't have a single doubt that she and Cully were right for each other.

So right that nothing could go wrong.

* * * * *

**This summer, the legend
continues in Jacobsville**

*Diana
Palmer*

A LONG, TALL
TEXAN SUMMER

Three **BRAND-NEW** short stories

This summer, Silhouette brings readers a special
collection for Diana Palmer's LONG, TALL TEXANS
fans. Diana has rounded up three **BRAND-NEW**
stories of love Texas-style, all set in Jacobsville,
Texas. Featuring the men you've grown to love from
this wonderful town, this collection is a must-have
for all fans!

*They grow 'em tall in the saddle in Texas—and
they've got love and marriage on their minds!*

Don't miss this collection of original Long, Tall Texans
stories…available in June at your favorite retail outlet.

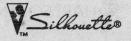

Look us up on-line at: http://www.romance.net

LTTST

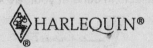

And the Winner Is...
You!

...when you pick up these great titles
from our new promotion at your
favorite retail outlet this June!

Diana Palmer
The Case of the Mesmerizing Boss

Betty Neels
The Convenient Wife

Annette Broadrick
Irresistible

Emma Darcy
A Wedding to Remember

Rachel Lee
Lost Warriors

Marie Ferrarella
Father Goose

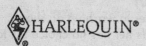 HARLEQUIN®  Silhouette®

Silhouette is proud to introduce
the newest compelling miniseries by
award-winning author

SUSAN MALLERY

TRIPLE TROUBLE

Kayla, Elissa and Fallon—three identical triplet sisters
are all grown up and ready to take on the world!

❊❊❊❊❊❊❊❊❊❊❊❊❊❊❊❊❊❊❊❊❊❊

In August: **THE GIRL OF HIS DREAMS**
(SE#1118)

Could it be Prince Charming was right in front of her
all along? But how was Kayla going to convince her
best friend that she was the girl of his dreams?

In September: **THE SECRET WIFE**
(SE#1123)

That Special Woman Elissa wasn't ready to throw in
the towel on her marriage, and she set out to show
her husband just how good love could be the second
time around!

In October: **THE MYSTERIOUS STRANGER**
(SE#1130)

When an accident causes her to wash up on shore,
the handsome man who finds her has no choice but to
take in this mysterious woman without a memory!

Don't miss these exciting novels...only from

Silhouette ®SPECIAL EDITION®

Look us up on-line at: http://www.romance.net   TRIPLE

Silhouette®

SPECIAL EDITION™

COMING NEXT MONTH

#1111 THE 200% WIFE—Jennifer Greene
That Special Woman!/Stanford Sisters
Abby Stanford always gave 200% to her family, her job…even to making cookies! And when she met Gar Cameron she knew that if he married her, she'd be the *perfect* wife. But Gar didn't want perfection…. He just wanted to love Abby 200%!

#1112 FORGOTTEN FIANCÉE—Lucy Gordon
Amnesiac Justin Hallwood felt inexplicitly drawn to beautiful Sarah Conroy and her toddler son. Would he regain his memory in time to start anew with the woman and child who were so deeply a part of his past?

#1113 MAIL-ORDER MATTY—Emilie Richards
Matty Stewart married her secret crush, Damon Quinn, for the good of his baby girl. But when the infant's custody became uncertain, they had to decide whether love alone could keep them together….

#1114 THE READY-MADE FAMILY—Laurie Paige
Harrison Stone felt trapped when he realized bewitching Isadora Chavez had duped him into marriage to safeguard her younger brother's future. Could this newfound family learn to trust in their hearts—and embrace honest-to-goodness happiness?

#1115 SUBSTITUTE BRIDE—Trisha Alexander
Rachel Carlton had secretly yearned for her twin sister's fiancé for years—and impulsively posed as David Hanson's bride! Now she needed to captivate her unsuspecting "husband" on their week-long honeymoon before the truth came out!

#1116 NOTHING SHORT OF A MIRACLE—Patricia Thayer
Widowed nurse Cari Hallen needed to believe in life—and love—again, and single father Nick Malone needed to open his heart to hope again, too. But it would take nothing short of a miracle to join these two unlikely people together….

From the bestselling author of
Iron Lace and *Rising Tides*

EMILIE RICHARDS

**When had the love and promises they'd shared turned
into conversations they couldn't face, feelings they
couldn't accept?**

**Samantha doesn't know how to fight the demons that
have come between her and her husband, Joe. But she
does know how to fight for something she wants: a child.**

**But the trouble is Joe. Can he accept that he'll never be the
man he's expected to be—and can he seize this one chance
at happiness that may never come again?**

"A great read and a winner in every sense of the word!"
—Janet Dailey

Available in June 1997
at your favorite retail outlet.

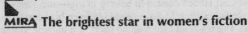

MIRA The brightest star in women's fiction